Diaries

of a

Nail Technician

Gossip heard in the salon never stays in the salon.

Ann Cedeño

INTRODUCTION

IF YOU WERE EVER A CLIENT OF MINE IN THE SALON,
you might recognize yourself or someone you know in this book.
I painstakingly changed the names, dates and details of events
so only the actual client will know when I am referring to them.

This book, not meant to expose anyone's secrets, is a sample
of the conversations that went on in the salon. For almost four
decades, I worked as a nail technician, listening to stories about
my clients and the people closest to them. I learned many valuable lessons worth sharing. Women are great teachers, but women
can be ruthless.

I began working as a nail technician in 1983. I wasn't even
old enough to drink or vote. While all my high school friends
were leaving for college, I was building my clientele. My career
became an education in women and the way they behave. It was
not what happened in my clients' lives, but how they reacted that
revealed who they were. Friendships, weddings, adoption, illness
and affairs were some of the topics discussed. I listened intently
to the stories.

"I bet you could write a book," clients often said.

I decided to give it a try.

Diaries of a Nail Technician, full of salon gossip, reveals the juicy secrets women have been telling their nail technicians and hairdressers for decades. Be careful what you say in public; you never know who's listening.

CHAPTER 1

Sonja Donato

IN 1985, SONJA DONATO WAS THE OWNER OF INDULGE Me, a salon in Plantation, Florida. She met Val Donato, her second husband when her three girls were small. Val owned a construction company and he bought homes in deplorable conditions in the best neighborhoods to renovate. Val and Sonja lived in the houses with the girls until they sold, and then they moved to the next house. Sonja hated all the moving around.

When Sonja walked into a room with her shoulders back and her head held high; it was impossible not to notice her. All of her friends looked to her for advice from clothing to skincare since she appeared to have all the answers. Once her girls left the nest, Val noticed that shopping at the mall was not enough to keep his wife busy.

"If you could own a business, what would it be?" Val asked. They were just sitting down to dinner. Sonja thought about it.

"I would love to own a salon." Spending hours in a salon every week, having her hair and nails done, was typical for Sonja.

Although she had no experience as a stylist, she was confident enough to learn the salon business.

Plantation desperately needed a full-service salon where women could get pampered. Val found the perfect location in a brand new shopping center. Indulge Me was the name Sonja chose for the salon, and everyone loved the idea. Indulge Me was a labor of love. Val put his heart and soul into designing and building a salon for his beautiful wife, but perhaps her beauty was her downfall. She was the perfect example of a bored housewife who was still young and desirable.

Sonja was almost 50, but she could have passed for at least ten years younger. There was no Botox in those years. Surgery was the only way to fix the damage done by time and the sun's intense rays. Everyone was tan, convinced the color gave them a youthful, healthy glow. Dr. Shulman, a well-known plastic surgeon in the area, gave Sonja a facelift before the salon opened. Her skin was pulled tight against her cheekbones like when she was in her 30s. The skin-perfecting makeup she applied each day took time and energy, and Sonja had both.

Women in the area passed by the salon while it was under construction to get a peek. Clothing was another passion of Sonja's, so Val added a clothing boutique at the entrance of the salon. The vestibule had steps that led to the boutique. The salon was brilliant in its design. The clients had to walk through the racks of clothing and accessories before arriving at the front desk to check-in. Captivated by the inventory in the boutique that was continually changing, the women would find it hard to leave without purchasing something. The boutique carried all the latest 80s fashions with shoulder pads in every blazer and glitzy belts covered in Swarovski crystals.

Only nail technicians and hairdressers with full clientele were hired before the salon's grand opening. Indulge Me had over 40 employees. They were so inundated with new customers, it was hard to accommodate them all. It was the perfect time for me to apply for a position as a nail tech. I was first impressed by the professionalism of the salon, and I knew I wanted to be a part of it. All the employees working at Indulge Me dressed in a sophisticated, edgy way.

When Sonja walked over to greet me, I noticed she was stunning; even her walk was flirtatious, and she had a mischievous look in her eyes. Her only job as the owner was to make sure things ran smoothly. Sonja led me to a nail station along the wall, where we sat down to talk. The impromptu interview took only minutes, and then Susie, another nail tech, joined us. Susie was friendly, but she was more interested in making plans for the evening with Sonja.

My last appointment is at 7:00," Susie told Sonja, "I need to have my hair done before we go."

Sonja hired me on the spot and wrapped up our meeting. The desk we were sitting at would become my new nail station. Robin, a gorgeous brunette in four-inch high Spanish Leather pumps, and Lori, a lesbian with long permed blonde hair, sat on either side of the station. I stopped at the front desk so that Jamie, Sonja's oldest daughter, could add me to the schedule. There was no such thing as social media. I was fortunate to have a list of my client's phone numbers from the previous salon. It paid to be friendly with the receptionist. Before I left, she copied all my client's phone numbers on a piece of paper and handed it to me. Jamie helped me call all my clients and set up new appointments.

Jamie was overweight but in a curvy sexy way. Her lips were full, and her eyes were big and brown. She had the same mischievous look I noticed in her mother. Jamie was married with a four-year-old son, but she admitted that she had a boyfriend on the side. We had no cell phones in those years. Her boyfriend could only reach her by calling the salon until she had a secret phone jack installed inside her closet at home with a different phone number. She plugged the phone into the hidden phone jack whenever her husband wasn't around.

At Indulge Me, the lights were bright, and 80s pop music played on the stereo system. The background noise was a constant hum between the blow dryers and the women's voices. The louder the noise from the blow dryers became, the women's voices rose in volume until their loud cackles of laughter sounded like chickens clucking on a farm.

The salon was intoxicating, and we made our jobs seem glamorous. We dressed every day like we were going to an event. Clients would say that they felt the need to get dressed up before coming in for an appointment because our hair and makeup were always impeccable, and our outfits were over the top. All the girls wore 80s glam, complete with shoulder pads and wide waist-cinching belts to accentuate our pre-baby bodies.

At all times, we had more than one young gay male hairdresser. They were moodier than the girls and they were the only ones who got away with walking out if a client upset them. The clients could be demanding. After finishing a particular client's nails in 25 minutes one day, she refused to get up.

"I am paying for the full hour," she said.

The regulars who came every week usually stayed long after their nails were dry to gossip. If they talked to each other, I wouldn't have to entertain them, and I could listen to their outrageous banter. I got to know them better and see them more often than some of my close friends. The manicures were almost secondary to the intense therapy sessions that happened every hour at my nail station. There are many "types" of women. I started to categorize them. The braggers were the most entertaining.

"Is that a new ring?" asked Carol.

"Yes, I got it for my anniversary," replied Marilyn.

"How many carats is it?"

"It's three carats." Carol held her finger out to show Marilyn her ring.

"Mine is four and a half."

While I was filing my clients' nails I would hear conversations across the room.

"We are cruising to the Mediterranean this summer."

"How many days?"

"14."

"Only 14? We went for 21 days last summer."

One day Michele walked by while I was doing Joan's nails.

"Hi, Michele, I haven't seen you in a while."

"We were away all summer."

"How is your son?"

"Fabulous, He's starting medical school."

"That's wonderful. Where?"

"Cornell. We are taking him there next Thursday to find him an apartment."

"Mazel tov," Joan said. Michele walked away, and Joan turned back toward me.

"Have you seen her son? He's hideous."

Many of the employees went out after work to Vinny's, a local restaurant and night club. Sonja would join them occasionally, and it wasn't long before she caught the attention of Jose, a good looking guy in his early forties.

Jose arrived at the bar around 9:00. He noticed Sonja immediately. Jose was there every week; he would have remembered Sonja if he ever saw her before. Jose could tell Sonja had money. The jewelry, the clothes, and the way she carried herself, it was easy to see. Was that a wedding ring on her finger? Married women made perfect girlfriends. No demands and no commitment. They even paid for dinner sometimes, happy to have someone paying attention to them.

Jose made his way through the crowd to where Sonja was standing with Susie and Annette. The bartender set three drinks down on the bar, and Sonja picked up her glass. Over the loud music, the bartender asked if Sonja wanted to start a tab.

"Yes," Sonja said. When she turned back around, she was face to face with Jose.

"Care to dance?" Jose asked. Sonja was caught off guard.

"I'm married."

"Then what are you doing here?"

"I'm here with my girlfriends," she said. It was shocking how handsome Jose was. He had dark hair, his eyes were bright blue, and he knew just how to flirt.

"It's only a dance," Jose said. Sonja looked at Susie and Annette. They both seemed impressed by how cute Jose was. Sonja took a long sip of her drink from the straw and then set the empty cup down on the bar and followed Jose out onto the dance floor. The DJ played "All Night Long" by Lionel Richie, and Sonja's head started to feel foggy from the vodka. Jose was an incredible dancer. Granted, he was 20 years younger than Val, but Val never enjoyed dancing. He only enjoyed making money, and lately, he worked most of the time. After the song ended, Jose walked Sonja back to the girls at the bar. Susie and Annette excused themselves to go to the ladies' room. Jose slipped a tiny baggie of cocaine into Annette's hand as she passed. He made sure Sonja didn't see, knowing she was not the type to be involved with anyone who did drugs. Annette and Susie were younger than Sonja, and Jose could tell they loved to party.

When Jose told Sonja that he owned an Auto Body Shop, she looked at his hands and could tell he was not a mechanic, and the shop was successful because he was wearing a new gold Rolex. She only ever dated successful men. Money was power, and without it, life was boring. As the bar emptied, Sonja went to pay the tab for herself and the girls. Jose moved her hand away and placed a few large bills on the bar, and they all walked out together. They arrived at Sonja's car first. It was a brand new Mercedes. Jose kissed Sonja right on the lips as the girls stood there with their mouths hanging open. Sonja slipped into the driver's seat and noticed the time. It was 2 a.m. Val would be furious with her for coming home late, but whatever grief she faced when she got home would be worth it. The night was one of the best nights of her life. As she pulled away, she saw Jose talking to Annette and Susie in the parking lot.

Quietly Sonja put her key in the lock on the front door. When she shut it behind her, it made the slightest click. She removed her shoes and walked toward her bedroom. Val was sleeping on the sofa, and he didn't stir. She took off her clothes and slipped under the covers; Val would stay asleep in the other room with any luck. She wanted to relive the whole evening in her mind. She closed her eyes and pictured how Jose kissed her by the car, and slowly slipped into darkness. In the morning, Sonja opened her eyes as Val walked into the bedroom.

"You got home late," Val said. He didn't admit he had no idea what time she finally showed up.

"Annette and Susie didn't want to leave." The room smelled like cigarette smoke from Sonja's clothes. As Val got into the shower, she jumped up, threw the outfit into a bag for the dry cleaner, and walked into the bathroom to remove last night's makeup.

Lately, Sonja had been going out more frequently. Val didn't like it when she went out without him, and he gave her the cold shoulder as he dressed for work. Pretending not to notice, Sonja made Val coffee and scrambled eggs. While he ate breakfast, she got into the shower to wash the smoke smell out of her hair.

The salon was full by the time Sonja arrived. Annette greeted her at the door.

"What an incredible night," Sonja said.

"Jose asked me to give you his number." Sonja took the number from Annette but had no intention of calling Jose. It seemed too forward, and she was married, after all. Sonja noticed the line to pay at the front desk. She checked her makeup in the mirror and walked over to help Jamie take payments and schedule appointments.

Sonja's eye lids felt heavy toward the end of the day. She was comfortably seated in the chair at the front desk. The clients seemed more needy than usual.

"Mom, you have a phone call," Jamie said.

"Who is it?"

"It's a guy." Sonja's heart began to pound; she picked up the extension in the boutique.

"Hello?"

"Hi." The voice was deep and raspy. Sonja knew it was Jose.

"The girls told me where to find you; I hope I didn't get you into trouble last night." Sonja didn't know what to say. "When can I see you again?" Jose asked.

"I'm not sure."

"I will be at Vinny's on Thursday."

Jose hung up, and Sonja walked out of the boutique, like the cat who just ate the canary.

"Who was that?" Jamie asked.

Sonja knew there was a good chance Annette or Susie would mention what happened, so she told Jamie everything; she was dying to tell someone. Jamie was not the biggest fan of Val. As a stepfather, he always treated her like a second class citizen. There was no love between them.

"Just be careful, Mom," Jamie said.

Slowly Sonja transformed into a different person. She went out with the girls all the time and began losing weight. She was no longer forfeiting having her hair or nails done when a paying customer was waiting; she started to put herself first. Her clothing became sexier as her weight loss increased. She began to leave during the day for extended lunch breaks, and one afternoon she even brought Jose into the salon for a haircut. Her behavior was reckless.

Claiming she needed space, Sonja went away with Jose for the weekend; Val had her followed, and her infidelity cost her everything. Once Sonja's husband found out about the affair, he was on a mission to destroy her and take back everything he ever gave her.

Arriving early one morning for work, Val and his son from his first marriage, Rob, greeted me at the door. I had only met Val once before, when he came into the salon with his crew to install chairs in the pedicure room. Rob looked like Val's bodyguard, tall and muscular, and in his early 30s. Jamie was gone, and in her place were two new receptionists standing behind the front desk. Val was no longer Jamie's stepfather, now that he divorced her mother; that was clear. The new receptionists, Eileen and Helene, had plenty of experience working in a busy salon.

We still booked all of our appointments in pencil on a massive oversized appointment book that was splayed open, and Eileen was studying it. As more employees walked in, Val explained he was taking over the salon. Val became the sole owner after the divorce. What would become of the salon? Could Val run it the way Sonja could? Determined to make it more successful without Sonja, he put every ounce of energy he had left into Indulge Me.

Val subleased the boutique. The hefty rent made up a portion of what he paid the shopping center every month. It was a smart business move on his part, and Joyce, a petite brunette with a pixie haircut, rented the space and began filling it with new merchandise. She went to school for fashion merchandising, and her father was funding her little endeavor. Joyce would take buying trips and come back with tons of outfits and accessories. Pleated pants with blazers and skirts with matching tops were some of the best sellers, and she always had earrings to complete the look. She only bought one outfit in each size so no one would see themselves coming and going. The clients couldn't wait to try the new clothing on. The stylists would have to go into the boutique to drag their clients out before they carelessly wandered into the dressing rooms during their appointment times. Time was always of the essence, and there wasn't a minute to spare. Any employee who dared to run late could upset the entire schedule.

Once Eileen saw how fast we could work, she started booking our appointments closer together, and we were scheduled to work from open to close. If we had a headache, Eileen brought us Tylenol, and if we were hungry, she ordered pizza. Eileen and Helene never turned away any paying customer. We worked on commission in those years, and our split was 55% of our total for the week plus our tips. We were all shocked by how much money we were making.

Everything was going smoothly until the police showed up at the salon one day. A client who had been getting her nails done with Susie was sitting in the chair at her station. The officers placed handcuffs on Susie and Annette and led them through the salon and out the front door to a waiting patrol car. Susie and Annette unknowingly sold cocaine to undercover female detectives posing as clients. Jose had been their supplier.

Annette was sitting on a long metal bench shivering inside the jail cell; it felt like 60 degrees in there. Why did they have to keep the temperature so cold? The female undercover detective who had been having her nails done by Annette for weeks walked by. The detective held up her hands, waving her long acrylic nails.

"How do I get these things off?"

Susie and Annette came back to work days later like nothing ever happened. Only in a salon could you get arrested at work and not be let go. In any salon, an owner would never fire a constant high earning employee for any reason. A salon's success depends highly on the employees and their clientele; without them, the salon would be empty.

Just when I thought I would never see Sonja again, she called me.

"Annie, would you mind coming to Jamie's house in the morning to do my nails? I am going away for a while."

I always liked Sonja and Jamie, and I was excited to see them. I wondered why Sonja needed her nails done on a Sunday as I drove to Jamie's house early in the morning with all of my supplies in a cardboard box. Jamie's husband opened the door and led me to the kitchen, where Jamie was telling her mother about her new job working as the receptionist in Dr. Shulman's Surgery Center.

Dr. Shulman performed amazing breast augmentations and facelifts, but he was known mostly for his noses. Sonja was drinking coffee, and three unopened shopping bags sat on the floor next to her. They were gifts she brought for Jamie.

"Where are you going?" I asked Sonja.

"My fiancé hired a private jet to take us to New York this afternoon."

Sonja broke up with Jose when she found out he was dealing drugs. Her new fiancé was an older gentleman who lived in a mansion in Boca Raton in the winter, and an apartment in New

York City in the summer. He was quite a bit older than Sonja; eighty years old, according to Jamie. Helping him put his shoes on in the mornings was a small price to pay for the lifestyle Sonja enjoyed now.

CHAPTER 2

Melissa Cohen

JAMIE SENT ONE OF THE NURSES FROM DR. SHULMAN'S Plastic Surgery Center to me when she needed a new manicurist. Melissa Cohen, a blonde with deep-set blue eyes, made a standing appointment the first time I met her and came in every Wednesday at 5:00 for more than a decade. I appreciated that she always knew what color polish she wanted. Red nails were popular in the 80s, and Melissa usually wore a light shade of red with a little orange in it called Cadillac Red. It could be daunting to help the indecisive clients pick out a polish.

Melissa owned a small townhouse and lived alone with the little poodle she named Peaches. The poodle was paper-trained and stayed in the kitchen all day, laying in the warm sunshine that came through the sliding glass doors. Melissa didn't envy her friends who lived with their husbands. Not everyone wants the same things in life. Melissa preferred being alone, not having to answer to anyone.

Prone to breakouts, Melissa's skin was fair and blotchy. Her dermatologist was always doing chemical peels on her to try to rectify the problem. She wore heavy makeup to hide the imperfections in her skin. Chanel made a skin-perfecting foundation, and Melissa splurged on the expensive brand, but she was too frugal to use it. She saved the Chanel makeup for special occasions and usually used the many samples she collected from the mall's cosmetic counters instead. The expensive foundation she bought would be rancid before she ever finished it. To say that Melissa was frugal was an understatement. She would go to the mall to spray the tester perfumes in the fragrance department on her wrists before going out, and then ask for the tiny sample bottles to take home. In the produce drawers of her refrigerator, she would hoard all the samples, and she had quite a collection.

Hardly spending any money, Melissa had paid off the townhome and accumulated a huge balance in her savings account. She found plenty of ways to save. Collecting napkins anytime she passed a dispenser; her toilet paper sat untouched in the bathroom. She had a water bottle that she squirted on herself after urinating, and then dried herself with the free napkin and stuck them in the garbage, only flushing the toilet when absolutely necessary.

From the outside of the townhome at night, it appeared that no one was home. Melissa only turned on a light when she had no other choice to save on electricity. The small television in her bedroom provided enough of a glow to light up the entire second floor. She spent almost every evening at home, perfectly happy to be alone.

Afraid of becoming overweight, like her mother and her sister were, Melissa jumped rope inside the townhouse for hours and counted every calorie she consumed. A small container of cottage cheese was her lunch most days. The Plastic Surgery Center where she worked was busy, and the girls had little time to eat. Every day after work, Melissa stopped to buy a rotisserie chicken for dinner, usually using a coupon. With the plastic utensils the restaurant provided, she ate the entire chicken at her kitchen table right out of the shallow paper dish it came in, saving the last few pieces for Peaches. When she finished, she collected the chicken's carcass in a plastic bag and carried it out to the dumpster to discard it. Melissa never had to wash a dish. Storage was limited in the townhouse so she folded her sweaters and jackets and stored them the dishwasher. The candy she kept in the freezer was her downfall. Milky Way bars, M&M's, and Life Savers filled the shelves.

Melissa's sister shared her love of candy, and the extra weight she carried had not stopped her from getting married and having children. Melissa adored her nieces and nephew and drove six hours to Jacksonville to visit them from time to time. They lived a few blocks from Melissa's parents and the whole family spent every holiday together. Occasionally, her parents wanted to come down to visit her, but she didn't like anyone staying in her house. Whenever they suggested it, Melissa made up an excuse to avoid a visit from them.

Every morning before work, she woke up early to get coffee at Dunkin' Donuts before doing three sets of push-ups and sit-ups. On the weekends, weather permitting, Melissa drove to the beach to walk on the boardwalk for exercise. When she finished her 5-mile walk, she would get a pizza slice from the pizza parlor's walk-up window. After enjoying the piping hot slice of pizza they served on a thin paper plate, she stood looking out at the ocean. She loved the balmy heat on her skin and the sounds and smell of the sea. Noisy seagulls flew overhead, always searching for bits of food on the sand. The waves crashed and then retreated in a constant ebb and flow. Her skin was dark, and her hair was sun-streaked, and under her jean shorts and T-shirt, she wore the same Gideon Oberson bikini that she had for over 10 years.

Melissa discarded the backpack containing her sneakers and running shorts on the warm sand and waded slowly past the crashing waves until she reached the sandbar's calm shallow water, spending a few minutes there to cool down. She never left without rinsing off the sticky sand and saltwater in one of the showers along the boardwalk. The hot sun almost immediately evaporated every last drop of water from her hair and her body as she headed back to the parking garage. Not even one grain of sand ended up in her car. Carefully she used a towel from her trunk to wipe down her legs and feet before she got back in so she wouldn't have to vacuum the floor mats.

At work, Dr. Shulman had the entire female staff wear a shade of pink scrubs every day. The uniform made dressing for work easy, and Melissa's whole clothing wardrobe hung unworn in the closet. When she came into the salon for her appointments, she was always wearing her scrubs. In all the years I did her nails, I rarely saw her wearing anything else.

A maid was the one splurge Melissa allowed herself. Once a month the pink scrubs and her bath towels were washed and then folded, and the sheets on the bed were changed to a crisp fresh set.

The patients Melissa took care of in the office loved her and always wanted to fix her up with someone they knew. The best way to meet someone in those years was by introduction. One night Melissa had a date. When the guy drove her home he ended up coming in for one last drink. Things got hot and heavy and as they were about to have sex on Melissa's bed she grabbed one of Peaches' pee-pee pads from the box. The guy heard a crunching sound in the dark as she slipped the pad under her bottom. She needed the sheets to stay clean so she wouldn't have to change them herself. I suspected that was why Melissa was still single at 47 years old.

I went into the surgery center one day for an appointment. It was so good to see Jamie in the office. Melissa was visiting her parents in Jacksonville.

"I'm surprised Melissa never got married," I said.

"Didn't she tell you?"

"Tell me what?" Melissa was a phone sex operator. She made a dollar a minute talking to men late at night. Talking to men on the phone for years, she had perfected her skills, often keeping them on the line for close to an hour at a time.

CHAPTER 3

Cheryl Tannenbaum

CHERYL TANNENBAUM, A GYNECOLOGIST'S WIFE, HAD her nails done every Thursday at 9 a.m. with my friend, Samantha. Debbie, one of the hairdressers, pulled up a rolling tray table and began applying color to Cheryl's roots while she had her nails done. I overheard Cheryl telling the girls that her husband had left her for his receptionist.

Before Beth became the receptionist and started sleeping with Cheryl's husband, Dr. Edward Tannenbaum, she was a teacher's assistant in an elementary school. She hated the job, but she needed it to pay her rent and support her shopping habit.

One morning Beth woke up out of a dream. Trying to recall the sordid details of the recurring dream about high school, she walked into the bathroom to remove the tampon she had inserted the night before. She wasn't bleeding anymore, and there was no sign of the tampon, but it had to be in there somewhere. During work that day, Beth checked to see if the tampon had resurfaced somehow, but nothing was there. A co-worker suggested she call her gynecologists office and ask what to do. Beth had never needed a gynecologist before, always using Women's Awareness for exams and birth control, so she asked her sister for advice.

Beth's sister, married to an orthopedic doctor, used Dr. Tannenbaum as her gynecologist. Beth called the office in a panic, and the nurse told her to come right in. Sitting in the exam room in a paper gown, she wondered if the doctor would think she was crazy. The door opened, and Edward entered the room looking handsome in his white lab coat over a pair of tight-fitting jeans and a polo shirt. His cologne was intoxicating. As he was examining Beth, he explained that a tampon couldn't get lost inside of her.

"Everything looks fine," the doctor said. "Maybe you thought you inserted a tampon, but clearly, you did not." Beth was embarrassed, and she sat up.

"You do need to start having a yearly exam," Edward said, and he instructed the nurse to set her up with an appointment. All-day long, he couldn't stop thinking about Beth. She was a beautiful girl with long dark hair, but that wasn't it. It was the way Beth looked up at him like he was God. At that moment, he realized that his wife had never looked at him like that. Even when they were first dating, Cheryl never seemed impressed by him, and he found himself fantasizing about Beth.

A week later, Beth showed up for her scheduled gynecological exam. Edward spent over an hour with her, asking about her family history and recording every detail. He had never spent so much time with a patient even on the first visit, but he had trouble pulling himself away. The feeling was mutual; Beth seemed to hang on every word he said.

"Where do you work?" Edward asked. Beth confided in him, explaining how the career choice she had made might be the wrong one.

"We are looking for a receptionist here if you are interested." As soon as the words left his lips, he knew he was asking for trouble.

"I would love to work in a doctor's office," Beth said. Edward had her write her phone number on a piece of paper. He put the number in his pocket and promised to call her so she could come in for a formal interview. Edward began to call Beth every day, and he hired her as his new receptionist after several long conversations. He was very generous, and as the receptionist in the office, she made twice what she previously made at the school. Edward loved having Beth in the office at the front desk.

The romance was over with Cheryl. They stayed together for the sake of their sons, but Edward was tired of living in misery. They hadn't had sex in over a year because Cheryl wasn't interested. Before long, the nurses seemed to notice something was going on between the doctor and Beth. At age 25, Beth was 26 years younger than Edward's wife, but it wasn't Beth's youth that attracted Edward; it was Beth's total admiration of him. Edward complained about his wife being distant and cold. Beth thought if she were married to him, she would be the best wife there ever was.

Only dating guys her age in the past, Beth never fell in love with any of them. The boys her age seemed so juvenile, now that she was spending time with a real man. Beth felt safe with Edward, and she found his manly hands and chest hair very sexy.

It was common for Edward to receive phone calls in the middle of the night when one of his patients went into labor, so Cheryl didn't suspect anything when he started sneaking out to see Beth. The first time Edward went to Beth's apartment, he brought a $150 bottle of red wine. She had never tasted such an expensive red blend. He suggested they watch a movie together on the sofa, but half-way through the film, they ended up in the bedroom. That night was the start of an ongoing affair.

Before the affair with Edward, Beth spent her evenings and weekends shopping at the mall. She bought entire wardrobes of clothing for a social life she did not have. At the end of the season, with most of it unworn and the tags still attached, she tried to return whatever the stores would take back to her maxed-out credit cards. The stores with the designer bags she was obsessed with had a strict 14-day policy to exchange purchases. An entire collection, in every size, sat untouched in her closet.

Edward and Beth spent hours together at Beth's tiny apartment. There was never any food in the refrigerator. Only Diet Coke and bottled water filled the shelves. Edward didn't need food when he was with Beth; they spent most of the time in her bed, planning a future together. When the subject of babies came up, Edward made it clear that he already raised two children and the last thing he wanted to do was start over. Traveling and retirement were the two things on his mind now, and he was not looking to veer off track.

The gifts Edward bought Beth swept her off her feet. Cheryl thought Edward was at a weeklong doctor's convention when he took Beth to New York. They wandered into the Chanel store. Edward let Beth pick out a bag to give her a taste of the life they could have together without any interruptions, like children.

When the car Beth had been driving since college began to have problems, Edward bought her a brand new BMW. He made sure the statements came to the office instead of the house.

Edward frequently took Beth to dinner in Miami. She had a new outfit she had been dying to wear. It would be perfect with her new Chanel bag and a pair of Valentino pumps. Edward felt so proud of her on his arm as they walked through the bar at Joe's Stone Crab. She was the youngest, most beautiful girl in the room.

Edward was sure they would blend into the crowd in Miami, and no one they knew would spot them, but one of Cheryl's friends was there with a few girls for a birthday celebration. The friend walked right by them to step outside and call Cheryl, but they never noticed, wrapped up in their own conversation.

"It's impossible!" Cheryl said. "Edward is at the hospital right now, delivering a baby." Deep down, Cheryl knew how ridiculous she sounded. She hung up the phone and got into her Mercedes. She planned to drive through the hospital parking lot to make sure Edward's Porsche was in the usual spot. When she couldn't find it, she began to panic. How could this be happening? Almost forgetting to put the car in park, Cheryl left the Mercedes and ran past security. The guard stopped her, and she explained that there was an emergency, and she needed to find her husband. The guard took control and called Labor and Delivery. When he hung up the phone, the guard claimed that Edward had not been there all day.

Edward always paid cash when he was out with Beth, careful not to raise any red flags with Cheryl, but he forgot to go to the bank that day. Luckily, he had just enough cash to cover the bill and the tip. Edward saw Cheryl's friend at the bar on the way out. The look on her face told Edward that he was in trouble. The hour-long car ride was torture. Cheryl was blowing up his phone; there were more than a dozen missed calls. He pulled into the parking lot of Beth's apartment complex.

"When will I see you?" Beth asked.

"I will call you," Edward said. He knew he had to face Cheryl. Maybe it was better, at least now she knew about the affair. The gas light had been on in the Porsche, and he stopped at a gas station, prolonging the confrontation he was about to have. He inserted his credit card in the slot at the pump. The card was denied. Edward tried his debit card, also rejected. He got into the car and drove home. Cheryl had reported all of the credit cards stolen.

Edward always came into the house through the garage, but nothing happened when he pressed the button to lift the door. Walking around the house to the back, he saw Cheryl on a lounge chair with a glass of wine in her hand. Cheryl knew that all of her friends would find out about the affair. She stood up and threw the wine glass at his head, but it fell to the ground, shattering.

"How dare you do this to me!"

Over the next few months, Edward had to contend with the divorce and the fact that half of his assets would now belong to Cheryl. Edward worked so hard to pay off the mortgage on their home, only to have Cheryl receive it free and clear in the divorce. Nothing would change financially for her or her children. Edward had to pay alimony and finish paying for the boys' education. One son was in college and the other a senior in high school. While Edward was busy with his girlfriend, the boys comforted their mother. They wanted nothing to do with their father.

Edward rented a house while he was sorting out his finances. He tried not to burden Beth with the details of his divorce. Only occasionally, Beth would see Edward on the phone outside, waving his hands in the air and yelling. After the incredibly stressful fights with Cheryl over money, he became moody. Beth comforted him and the nights with her made up for everything.

Edward gave Beth days off from the office to shop and go to lunch with her sister. When she came home in the afternoons from shopping, he loved how she thanked him for all the purchases. It was worth every penny to see Beth so thrilled.

In the middle of all the drama, Beth was feeling nauseous, and her breasts felt tender. She was on the pill, but she frequently forgot to take it. On Saturday, while the office was closed, Edward did a pregnancy test. They were both genuinely shocked by the positive result. Edward's retirement and travel would have to wait another twenty years, but he thought it was a small price to pay to share a life with someone who truly made him happy.

The next day Edward bought a perfect two carat diamond solitaire for Beth. They drove down to the beach where he proposed to her on a blanket under the stars. Beth never worked another day in the office. She was busy making the home she shared with Edward cozy and comfortable. She chose furniture and dishes she had always admired from Bloomingdales, and the rental house looked picture perfect.

Edward and Beth were married at the courthouse with only Beth's sister and her husband present at the ceremony. The two couples rode in a limousine to Miami, where they dined at The Forge to celebrate before the happy couple left for a two-week honeymoon in Europe. Besides a little morning sickness, Beth had a fabulous time on the trip. Edward showed her all his favorite spots in Venice. He felt personally responsible for her happiness. Like taking a child to Disney World for the first time, Edward saw everything through Beth's wide expressive eyes, and he loved every minute of it. When they got home, reality set in.

Although Edward was a doctor with a very successful practice, the money he made wasn't endless. He was spreading himself very thin, between paying Cheryl and supporting his new household. Edward eventually found out about Beth's shopping obsession and her $60,000 in debt. He paid the debt and assumed that would be the end of her extravagant spending, but it was only the beginning.

After the first trimester of her pregnancy, Beth loved to go to the office to use the ultrasound machine to see the baby in her stomach. The other girls in the office were jealous of her, ending up with the handsome doctor. Still, when they saw Beth, they pretended to be interested as they gathered around to see the baby on the screen. She was acting like she was the first girl ever to get pregnant.

Everywhere she went, Beth saw babies. Had there always been so many babies around, and she never noticed before? At the mall new mothers were pushing costly strollers with perfectly dressed infants sleeping like little angels. The babies looked so cozy in their designer onesies and blankets to match. Beth couldn't wait to have her own bundle of joy to show off.

Edward was hoping for a girl after raising two boys with Cheryl, but the later sonograms revealed that the baby was a boy. Beth was busy buying all the things she would need, and the closet in the nursery had baby boy outfits in every size.

Beth was tired toward the end of her pregnancy, and she would fall asleep reading "What to Expect When You're Expecting" every night. The plan was to breastfeed the baby for the first six months to ensure he got all the necessary nutrients. She prepared by setting up a bassinet in the master bedroom so she could easily scoop him up for feedings in the middle of the night.

Elliott was born by C-section after 24 hours of labor. They named the baby after Edward's father, who recently passed away. Elliott seemed like the perfect infant eating and sleeping all day long in the hospital, but he never stopped crying once they got home. Edward hired a baby nurse, but to feed him, the nurse had to hand him over to Beth. The nurse helped bathe the baby and change his diapers, and once Beth recovered from surgery, they let the nurse go. Edward needed sleep. The baby was up all night. When Edward's alarm went off in the morning, he could barely open his eyes.

"Were your other boys fussy?" Beth asked. Edward could hardly remember. It was so long ago, and Cheryl always got up in the night with the babies. Finally, Edward had to move to a spare room, and he couldn't help feeling envious that the baby had taken his place with his new bride.

When it was time to see the pediatrician, Beth asked Edward to take her and the baby to the appointment. She didn't feel comfortable driving the baby by herself and then transferring him into the stroller. Edward had never been to a pediatrician's office before. As they sat in the waiting room filled with crying babies, Edward's chest felt heavy, and he had to try to control his breathing so he wouldn't have a full-blown panic attack. Starting over at this age was brutal. Maybe he just needed a good night's sleep.

The pediatrician suggested more protein in Beth's diet. The baby may be hungry at night. Beth didn't cook, but the one thing Edward could make was steak on the grill, and Beth loved steak. After work, Edward stopped at the market and picked up steak and broccoli. When he got home, Beth was waiting for him to hold the baby while she showered. Elliott fell asleep in his arms, and he began steaming broccoli and grilling the steak. Beth set the table, but as soon as they sat down to eat, Elliott started screaming and she jumped up.

"You have to quit jumping every time he cries!" Edward said.

Tears stung Beth's eyes. She felt like a failure. The books said that the baby would sleep most of the time and only eat every three hours, but Elliott was not cooperating. If only they could get through the baby stage, their marriage could make it through anything. Beth finally conceded to give the baby formula, and he was sleeping better during the day but still up at night. They hired a full-time nanny to help.

Beth started to shop for the groceries now that she had someone to watch the baby, and Edward continued to prepare the steak dinners a few nights a week. Edward gave Beth a debit card for essentials with plenty left over to get a few things every week at the mall for herself, but now that Beth was a doctor's wife, she fully intended to act like one. The mall became her escape from the baby. Now when new mothers walked passed pushing strollers, she noticed dark circles under their eyes, which she hadn't seen before.

Beth picked out a stack of clothing and shoes that totaled over $2,000 in Nordstrom one afternoon. Edward had asked her not to spend so much money earlier in the week when he came home from the office in a bad mood; the pressure to pay for everything was becoming overwhelming. Cheryl, the nanny, the office staff; everyone was waiting to get paid. One of Nordstrom's friendly salespeople suggested Beth open a credit card in her name. To her surprise, she received a $10,000 limit.

Walking into the house after a long day at the office, Edward sometimes found himself daydreaming about one of the dinners Cheryl used to prepare, complete with a homemade pie for dessert. Is that a cherry pie I smell? Edward thought, as he almost tripped on a squeaky baby toy on the way to the kitchen. Then he saw the cherry-scented candle burning on the kitchen counter. Beth was napping on the couch in front of the television while the nanny was bathing the baby. Edward found the steak in the refrigerator and started heating the grill.

Edward's big toe had been throbbing all day. He took off his shoe and saw that it was red and swollen. The pain was excruciating, and it felt like a broken toe, but Edward recognized that it was Gout (A build-up of uric acid). He remembered his father had Gout, and now he had it, probably from eating so much steak. Edward was feeling old for the first time in his life.

I had no idea who Beth was the first time she had her nails done with me. Everyone was staring at this tall beauty as she walked through the salon dripping in jewelry. She sat down at my desk. She wanted a full set of acrylic nails for a wedding she was attending.

"Who's getting married?" I asked.

"My stepson," Beth said. She looked too young to have a step-son old enough to be married. I was thinking about the poor ex-wife. If my ex-husband walked into my son's wedding with this stunning young girl on his arm, I would smash a wine bottle and slit my wrists in front of the guests with one of the shards of glass. No matter how beautiful a fifty-year-old woman is, there is no way she could compete with this dark-haired beauty. No airbrush in the world can paint on a twenty-year-old complexion.

I was still doing Beth's nails every other week when Elliott turned three. She brought in an oversized tote, filled with designer bags that she wanted to sell. She had gotten into trouble with her Nordstrom credit card, maxing it out. Afraid to tell Edward about the large balance after promising to stop spending so much money every month, she hoped to sell enough for the minimum amount due. Clients and nail techs gathered around, pulling one bag out after the other—every bag sold at a fraction of what she originally paid for them.

"Beth?" I heard someone say.

"Hello, Cheryl," Beth said. I wondered how they knew each other.

When Beth left the salon, Cheryl told us how she was the former receptionist in the office who had stolen her husband. Neither one had any idea the other came to our salon.

It was not uncommon for women who knew each other to meet in the salon. Our salon was the most popular in the area. My clients often asked me to check the schedule to make sure another client wouldn't be in the salon while they were. Former wives, mothers-in-law, and friends dodged each other all the time.

Cheryl was still attractive. She easily could have found some-one new to spend her life with, but she never remarried. She couldn't let go of the anger she had toward Edward, and it wouldn't allow her to move on.

The next time Beth came in, I noticed a tiny baby bump. Although she seemed thrilled, I wondered what Edward thought about yet another child.

CHAPTER 4

Rhonda Skolnick

RHONDA SKOLNICK, MY CLIENT FOR MANY YEARS, had two boys, Seth and Garrett. One was adopted, and one was her natural child. Only Rhonda would know if it's possible to love the adopted son, Seth, as much as the natural one, but I suspect she did.

Rhonda and her sister Janet owned a specialty gift store in the mall, and they came to the salon together after work every Thursday. Rhonda was the more attractive sister, purely because she loved makeup and designer clothing. Dressed in a stunning outfit and a pair of Gucci pumps, Rhonda sat down next to her sister to have her nails done with me one afternoon.

Some clients wanted to talk about themselves the entire appointment, non-stop, without taking a breath. I barely had to say a word, and their voices become so soothing I started to daydream. Only after they asked me a question would I snap back into the moment. Clients should talk about themselves, and the nail techs should listen, not the other way around. Some stylists got caught up in recounting their lives week after week. They began a blow by blow account of the events in their personal lives as soon as the client was comfortably seated. It could have been a single girl dating different guys, and the stories are light and entertaining, or a married employee who wanted to complain about her husband and her life at home. Always interested in the topic of adoption, since I was adopted, I asked Rhonda if her son, Seth, ever considered finding his birth mother.

"Why would Seth want to search for someone who gave him away?" Rhonda asked defensively. It wasn't possible anyway because Rhonda burned his adoption papers the day they were signed. Seth's chances of finding his birth mother with no leads at all went literally up in flames. I could sympathize with how Rhonda felt. She wanted to forget her son ever had a birth mother to begin with, who wouldn't?

"Seth loves Rhonda, and he would never hurt her by searching for his birth mother," Janet added. I didn't know what to make of that statement. I certainly wouldn't want to hurt my mother either, but why would it have hurt her? Isn't it normal to wonder where you came from if you were adopted?

Janet had three daughters who grew up with Rhonda's boys, and the five cousins were very close. They each went away to college and then came back home to marry and have families of their own.

While Rhonda's son, Seth, was in college, his girlfriend cheated on him, and the break-up was devastating. They had been dating since high school, and Rhonda was sure the two would be married one day. Rhonda couldn't get her boys married soon enough; she wanted grandchildren in the worst way. In the salon, Rhonda spotted the shampoo girl, Denise, from across the room.

Denise and I were close friends. She had long straight dark hair and a perfect figure. Denise went to cosmetology school to be a hairdresser but began as an assistant, working hard to get her confidence up. Rhonda knew Seth would like her.

"Is she Jewish?" Rhonda asked me.

"Her father is," I said. That seemed to be good enough. I called Denise over and introduced her to Rhonda and Janet. Rhonda asked Denise if she had a boyfriend, and when she said no, Rhonda asked if she would like to meet her son.

"Sure?" Denise said, a little hesitant. Rhonda asked me for a piece of paper so she could write down Denise's phone number. When Rhonda and Janet left Denise sat down at my desk.

"You should go out with him," I said. "Seth comes from a great family, and he's adorable." Rhonda and Janet had been clients of mine for years already, and I knew any girl would be lucky to marry into their family.

Denise and Seth began dating. She was impressed by the home Seth lived in with his parents. Her upbringing was completely different than his. Denise's father left when she was young, and her mother had to raise her and her sister alone. She wasn't used to the lifestyle that Seth had always taken for granted. His parents bought him a brand new Corvette when he turned 16 and got his driver's license. She was working at the salon, saving money for a down payment on a car, borrowing her mother's car if she needed to drive somewhere.

Denise was sweet and respectful. While Seth was playing video games, Rhonda offered to take Denise shopping. Arriving at the Boca Town Center, Denise was surprised they were not going to the local mall. Her mother worked hard as a waitress in a steak house for years and simply didn't have the money to spend on the luxury items from these high-end stores.

Walking into the shoe department in Saks Fifth Avenue, Denise noticed one of the salespeople gave Rhonda a familiar nod and walked over to greet them. Rhonda proudly introduced

Denise, who, despite her simple attire, stood out in a crowd. Wearing a simple pair of jeans with a white T-shirt and a cropped cardigan, she turned heads as she walked by. She was so thin that her hip bones protruded through her jeans and though she was already over five and a half feet tall, her pumps had three-inch heels. She stood like a model on the runway.

The salesman brought over a few pairs of shoes to try on. Rhonda adored a good pair of shoes; she knew the right pair of shoes could turn your life around. Catching a glimpse of the price marked on the bottom, Denise felt uncomfortable trying on the Dior strappy sandals Rhonda picked out for her.

"Do you love them?" Rhonda asked. Denise never wanted to take them off; they felt so good on her feet.

"I love them, but they are so expensive," Denise said. Rhonda handed her credit card to the salesman.

"My treat," Rhonda said. Denise was shocked by how generous Rhonda was with her.

She hugged her boyfriends mother to thank her. The day was lovely; they both felt comfortable sharing secrets about themselves with each other. After traipsing through a few more stores, they ended the shopping spree in Neiman Marcus so that Rhonda could take Denise to the restaurant upstairs for lunch.

There were so many firsts for Denise that day. Who knew this little restaurant even existed? It was like a secret hideaway upstairs in the far corner of the store for only a select group of people. When they were seated with shopping bags flanking their chairs; the waiter brought them each over a glass of water and a popover with strawberry butter.

Rhonda told Denise cute stories about Seth when he was a baby, and Denise felt like she had known Rhonda forever. Denise thought the waiter was coming back to take their order from the menu, but he appeared with two tiny cups of chicken broth consommé instead. She took a tiny sip and thought the broth tasted like Thanksgiving dinner. They both ordered glasses of Chardonnay and identical salads with a warm salmon filet on top.

Later, Denise would describe the day to her mother. Her mother seemed less than impressed by it all. Who were these people to come along and sweep her daughter off her feet by showering her with expensive gifts?

Soon enough, Denise's single mother, Anna, met Seth's entire family. Seth proposed to Denise after only dating six months. Rhonda gave him one of her diamonds, and they took it to a jeweler to have it put into a setting. The jeweler took a look at the stone through a loupe.

"Lucky girl," the jeweler said.

The stone was over two carats and passed down to Rhonda from her grandmother. Rhonda helped Seth pick a simple setting in platinum with a baguette on either side, and he surprised Denise that night at dinner, slipping the ring into her champagne glass. The next afternoon, Rhonda called Anna to congratulate her and invite her to their home for a champagne toast. When Anna arrived with Denise's older sister, she was careful to park her car out of sight after the guard at the gate let them in. Anna felt her little Toyota didn't measure up.

Always friendly and smiling, Rhonda's husband greeted them at the door, and he made them feel warm and welcome. Laughter was coming from the oversized dining room where the entire family sat. Janet was there with her husband and her three girls and two of their boyfriends.

Denise and Seth were in the center of the room, and when they saw Anna, they both walked over together and kissed her hello. Since they first started dating, Seth called Anna to let her know if he would be bringing Denise home late, and he always asked Anna her opinion when he wanted to buy a gift for Denise.

Denise looked stunning in a simple black dress and the Dior heels. Anna was happy for her daughter, marrying into such a wealthy family, but at the same time, maybe a little jealous that she didn't choose the same. Rhonda insisted on giving the kids an engagement party for the family at the end of the month at her country club.

"Please feel free to invite your family," Rhonda told Anna, "I just need a headcount."

The engagement party was as fancy as any wedding. The country club had a round room off the main entrance called the library with dark wood walls and soft lighting. I had been to a smaller party in this room before, but Denise and Seth's engagement dinner was in the main ballroom overlooking the golf course. We found our place setting at the long table, and a waiter took our drink order. It was still daylight when we arrived, and we had a perfect view of the sun setting in the distance. There were over 50 people at the party, and 45 were Rhonda's guests. I could see Denise's mother, between all the fresh-cut white roses, at the other end of the table, looking slightly uncomfortable.

Rhonda and her husband tried to include Anna in the celebration as best they could. They had her stand as they toasted Seth and Denise, and everyone wished them a wonderful future together.

Every holiday included the two sisters with their husbands and all five children who were encouraged to bring whoever they were dating. That way, it was easy to see if they fit into the family. Even a simple dinner was festive with so many family members. The girl cousins, usually not easily won over, grew fond of Denise. They were all asked to be bridesmaids at the wedding, and Denise's sister was her maid of honor.

Anna insisted on planning her daughter's wedding herself. She reluctantly allowed Rhonda to pay for her own guest's dinners because they had far more guests, but Anna paid for the band and the venue. Anna and her aunt made all the centerpieces for the tables, and no florist could have done a better job. The aunt once worked for a florist, and she had done many weddings. Rhonda asked to see the room where the reception was going to be on the morning of the wedding.

"Are they going to cover the chairs?" Rhonda asked Denise. Denise felt very uncomfortable telling Rhonda that her mother spent more than she set aside for the wedding already.

"Ask your mother if she would mind if I pay for chair covers. These chairs are ugly," Rhonda said. Denise stepped away to call her mother. She hoped Rhonda couldn't hear Anna screaming into the phone. Anna's patience had finally run out. Denise pushed the phone against her head to stifle her mother's voice, but it was impossible.

Rhonda didn't care if she hurt anyone's feelings; there was no way she would feel embarrassed in front of her friends at her son's wedding. Everything needed to be perfect. The venue Anna chose, within her budget, was average looking, and Rhonda was determined to spice it up. She ordered and paid for covers for all of the chairs, and while she was at it, she had fabric draped on the walls and ceiling with up-lighting, casting a pink glow in the room. It cost her plenty at the last minute, but it transformed the otherwise plain space.

The past year had been a dream come true for Denise, and she wanted her mother to be happy for her. Denise tried hard to enjoy the moment and not feel guilty about it.

When Denise announced she was pregnant five months after the wedding, there was another celebration, but Anna declined the invitation. A first grandchild for Rhonda was a dream come true, but Anna was more worried about Denise's sister, who was also pregnant. Anna's oldest daughter wasn't married, and her boyfriend already had a wife and children.

Anna was too busy working and paying bills to be much help to Denise. Rhonda was there for her, though. They went shopping together and filled the entire nursery in Seth and Denise's new home. Denise no longer worked at the salon; she spent her days preparing for the baby.

One afternoon Denise saw a documentary on adoption, and she encouraged Seth to search for his birth mother. Seth had no interest, but he let Denise explore the idea if she wanted to. She had plenty of time on her hands, even after the baby was born. Rhonda hired a baby nurse for her in the beginning, and after that, a full-time nanny. Rhonda shopped for gifts for the baby, finally having a girl to spoil after raising only boys. Denise was also like the daughter she never had until she asked Rhonda about Seth's adoption. Denise presented it carefully, claiming she only wanted to know Seth's medical history. Offended, Rhonda let her know this was out of the question. Denise couldn't understand why it was such a secret, but she quickly dropped the subject, not wanting to upset Rhonda, knowing where her bread was buttered.

As soon as the baby started preschool, Denise became pregnant again with another girl. The family was thrilled to have these first two babies, and Seth's brother and cousins quickly followed suit, getting married, and having one baby after the next. The family was growing.

In Denise and Seth's house, it was all about the baby girls. The role of wife and mother was something Denise always dreamed of as a little girl, and here she was with everything she ever wanted. Seth tried to be attentive, but when he wasn't working or playing golf with his brother, he watched television and played video games. Denise had to make all the decisions when it came to raising the girls, so she looked to Rhonda for advice.

Suddenly Rhonda began to lose weight without trying. She always struggled with her weight, and high school was the last time Rhonda remembered weighing so little. I could tell she was trying to enjoy her new size by buying beautiful outfits to show it off, but she was afraid something might be wrong. Her doctor ordered a battery of tests.

When the tests came back the doctor asked Rhonda to see him in his office. Rhonda, her husband, and Janet squeezed into the tiny, dimly lit room where the doctor was seated at his desk with the test results in front of him. As many times as the doctor delivered bad news, it never got any easier. Rhonda had ovarian cancer, and it had already spread.

Rhonda's husband refused to accept that his wife would die, and he flew her all over the country to specialists. They all agreed that treatment would buy her some time, but she wouldn't last the year. The sisters had always been so close, raising their children together and working side-by-side every day at the store. It was hard to picture one without the other.

The harsh chemo treatments made Rhonda so sick she eventually stopped coming to the salon. I went to her house to do her nails. The house was quiet when the cleaning girl opened the front door, and I stepped into the foyer. On the coffee table in the living room was a family photo from her niece's wedding. All five children stood in the picture with their spouses. Both sets of parents sat in chairs in front of them. In the photo Rhonda was wearing a designer dress she flew to New York to find. It made me sad to think that she may not make it, and this family would have to go on without her.

I was nervous about seeing Rhonda, but she looked as beautiful as ever when she came out of her bedroom and sat down in the kitchen. Her mood was light and happy, but she was thinner than the last time I saw her. She talked about the day I introduced her to Denise. Little did we know that Denise and Seth would have two beautiful daughters together. I'm so happy she lived long enough to see them. That day would be the last time I saw her.

After the funeral, everyone was standing outside of the funeral home. Aunt Janet looked at Seth.

"It killed your mother when you wanted to search for your birth mother," Janet said. Seth was offended by his Aunt's comment, and it marked the start of the family drifting apart.

Rhonda's husband divided most of Rhonda's designer handbags and jewelry among Denise and her other daughter-in-law. Special instructions for two loose diamonds were in Rhonda's safety deposit box with notes for her granddaughters to read someday. Not wanting to leave her nieces out, Rhonda asked that her husband let them each chose one of her expensive watches.

One of the nieces, Abby, was a pharmaceutical rep working for a well-known drug company. She was the top salesperson every month. Abby made considerably more money than her husband and liked to remind him every chance she got. Abby's husband, David, was sick of how she belittled him, and David called Denise to confide in her about his marriage. He told her if it wasn't for their two boys, he would have left Abby.

Abby regularly sent samples from the drug company to her college roommate. No one would have known except that she mailed them using the companies prepaid label. Abby got a message to come to the office for questioning. She wasn't too worried. After all, she made a ton of money for the company, and she wouldn't be easy to replace. Abby's boss fired her on the spot.

Denise listened while David complained about Abby and tried to offer advice, but the conversations got more frequent, and they were less and less about Abby. Denise and David became confidants, and they found they had a lot in common. David started calling Denise every day, and it was a nice distraction. She was flattered that he was interested in her and what she had to say.

The young mothers Denise met at the temple preschool she enrolled the girls in were not her friends. Maybe it was Denise's insecurities when they asked where she went to college? Sensing she was different than they were, they never gave her a chance. It was possible they were afraid their husbands would notice her exotic beauty. They rarely invited Denise to any of the parties they threw.

Saturday nights when Rhonda was alive, consisted of dining in the most expensive restaurants. She always made reservations for herself and her husband and always included both sons and their wives. She even paid for the babysitters so her daughters-in-law could enjoy themselves without interruption. Wearing her latest purchases from Neiman Marcus, Denise ran into the moms from the preschool who shunned her during the week. It was Denise's turn to walk by them without giving them the time of day.

David continued to call Denise daily, and he found excuses to see her. He even met her at Starbucks on occasion to talk, knowing she went there every morning after she dropped the girls off at school. One of Abby's friends saw them together and ran back to Abby to tell her. David tried to say they just happened to run into each other that day, but Abby checked the phone records and discovered that Denise and David had been speaking several times a day for hours. Abby showed up crying to her parent's house, and her father was incensed.

Denise was home alone, preparing dinner before she left to pick up the girls from preschool when someone started banging on her front door. Through the peephole, she saw Seth's Uncle's angry face. She quickly crouched down so he wouldn't realize she was there. Thank God, she parked her new car in the garage.

Denise was shaking as she ran up the stairs. Her bedroom window had a perfect view of the front entrance, and when she looked down, she saw that Seth's Uncle's face was beet red from yelling. It seemed like forever before he finally gave up and left.

Seth got a call at work from his Uncle asking him to control his wife. Seth wasn't willing to lose his wife; he just lost his mother. Seth believed Denise when she said she only listened to David's complaints and offered him solutions to his marital problems. Promising never to speak to David again, Denise professed her love for Seth, and the marriage that had become complacent became passionate once again. Denise wasn't stupid. She knew her life was good, and the last thing she wanted to do was get a divorce.

Abby and David divorced. David couldn't convince Abby that the whole thing was innocent, and he didn't try very hard. He wanted out. With Rhonda gone, the two families that were once so close became sworn enemies. If Rhonda could see them now, she would be heartbroken.

Denise and Seth remained together and had a third daughter the next spring. The third daughter looked nothing like the other two.

CHAPTER 5

Maricel Torres

MY HUSBAND, ANGELO, AND I MOVED TO OUR FIRST home in Weston in 1996 with our two children. The builder promised we would be living in the house 10 months from the time they started building, and he had delivered. I continued to work as a nail technician in Plantation for the next 10 years, for fear of losing my clientele. Plantation is where I had worked most of my career, but I kept thinking what a pleasure it would be to work closer to home. Ten years later I finally made the move.

Wild Hare, located in the Weston Town Center, was one of the top salons in Weston in 2006. I booked an appointment to have my hair done by the owner so I could check it out. No one will know me, I thought, as I dressed for my appointment. I would look like any other Weston housewife.

Weston is quite a destination. Over 63,000 people lived in this master planned suburban community. On Bonaventure Boulevard landscapers could be seen daily trimming and fertilizing the endless plants and shrubs while men in white trucks pressure cleaned the curbs that lined the streets.

"Only in Weston," I would comment to my daughter, when we drove around the area. Nowhere else had I seen roads so pristine. Pleasantville was my nickname for the city that looked so perfect.

Weston was built by Arvida (known for developing Walt Disney World), which explained the fairytale atmosphere and the constant upkeep. Where else could you spot men hanging from lifts to pressure wash the light poles?

Weston was mostly self-contained, meaning no one needed to drive through Weston to get anywhere else. If someone was in Weston, it was usually because they lived or worked there. And many of the people who lived there preferred not to leave the bubble, whenever possible.

Landscaped berms ran down both sides of the streets, hiding any retail stores or medical buildings deemed eyesores from the traffic. The berms dropped back down intermittently revealing picturesque views of glimmering lakes and sunsets as perfect and pleasing as a fine oil painting in a museum.

Crime was virtually non-existent in Weston. The residents were out anytime of the day or night on bike paths that ran parallel to the street. Athleisure clad energetic 30-somethings cycled, ran and walked their dogs.

Wild Hare was at one end of the Town Center surrounded by shops and restaurants. Residents walked between the shops and down the main street, covered in brick pavers. I parked my SUV and walked through the open doors of the salon. It was June, and in Florida, the heat was oppressive. I wondered how the salon felt so cool inside with the doors wide open, but it was a very inviting feel. I walked up to the front desk where a girl who looked like a model named Mary asked me my name.

"Ann Cedeno," I said. "I have a 10:00 with Jean Paul." Mary told me to get shampooed and Jean Paul would be right out.

"Hello!" Jean Paul said.

He looked at me, and I could tell he didn't know if he had ever cut my hair before. He walked me to his station. I told him his salon was lovely, and that it was my first visit to save him the embarrassment of trying to awkwardly figure out if he knew me. We started to chat while he cut my hair and out of the corner of my eye I saw a familiar face barreling toward me.

"Annie!!" I kind of recognized this girl as someone I had worked with before. She was wearing all black so I knew she was an employee and she walked from the direction of the nail department.

"Hi!" I said. I couldn't remember her name.

"Jean Paul, this is Annie! She does the most incredible nails!" Jean Paul spoke with a heavy accent.

"Why don't you come work for me?" Little did he know that was my plan all along.

"I need to give notice."

"Fine! Start whenever you want!" I promised to send Mary my client list so she could begin the painful process of notifying my clients.

Two weeks later I started working at Wild Hare. The public schools in Weston were the best in the county and the reason that many young couples with children moved to the area. My son was in 6th grade in the local middle school and my daughter was a senior at Cypress Bay High School, rated one of Florida's top high schools. More than half of my clientele followed me to my new location in Weston, and Mary booked me with new clients when I had an opening. Gone were the days of Eileen and Helene walking a new client over to a stylist to introduce them. Mary never left her chair, and seemed annoyed whenever she had to move the magazine she was reading to the side to accept payment or book an appointment.

My second day working in Weston, I met Maricel Torres, an attractive Latin woman in her early 60s who was legally blind. Maricel was upset. Veronica, the nail tech whom I didn't recognize, did her nails the week before, and she was having a reaction. Maricel told Veronica she was allergic to acrylic, but apparently Veronica gave her acrylic anyway and told her it was gel. I had time, so I redid her nails. I got the feeling Veronica was sorry she ever spoke to me.

Maricel booked a standing appointment with me every other Tuesday at 11:00. Her vision impairment was not obvious; she was much too vain to walk with a cane, and she pretended to see as she made her way through the salon. The main problem with her loss of vision was that she could no longer drive. Even if there were taxis or public transportation in the city of Weston, it wouldn't solve Maricel's problem. She needed someone to be her eyes for her. She couldn't locate things on a shelf in the grocery store without help, and she was extremely particular. She would starve before she would consider taking a bite of anything but the most sought after food available.

Maricel must have always been difficult judging from her stories. Her husband left her years before, for a younger woman when her son, Gus, was eleven, and she managed somehow to push away her only child with her combative behavior.

Maricel had one sister who still lived in Venezuela, where Maricel was from. She hadn't spoken to her sister in years. Maricel and her sister had a falling out when their father passed away years ago over money, and they never spoke again. Frequently that was the case. Money caused so many problems between families. The only friends Maricel had were not her friends; they were the people she hired to help her shop. Whenever she ran into one of the many Weston residents who spoke Spanish, Maricel would approach them.

"I need someone to help me read my mail and take me shopping." When they pulled up to her house worth over $1,000,000 that she lived in alone, they assumed she would compensate them significantly for their time, but they would be wrong.

Maricel would always find a new person to drive her to the salon to have her nails done. Before the nail appointments, they read her mail for her and wrote out checks for various utilities and credit cards. She needed help organizing her things in her home so they would be easier for her to find when she was there alone. Chanel lipsticks, lip pencils, and nail polishes sat together in zip lock bags, so she didn't mistakenly wear the red lipstick with the pink nail polish. The bags were labeled with a Sharpie in large enough writing for her to see. She always brought her own polish with her to the salon.

"Check to see that they put the right ones together." Maricel asked me to read the small print on each item in the bag. She never trusted any of the people she hired.

After her nail appointment, there would be endless errands to run: the dry cleaners, the bank and the pharmacy. Only at the end of the day, when the assistants were so tired and tortured from her, would she take them to eat at a fancy restaurant that served only the finest cuts of steak, and that would be their payment for the entire day. I'm sure they would have preferred cash, but this was the only chance Maricel had to dine out at a restaurant.

Maricel loved red meat. It wasn't unusual for her to order a 22-ounce cowboy steak and devour the entire thing in one sitting after an appetizer of beef carpaccio. Food seemed to be her only pleasure, and nothing was ever good enough. The markets in the area had perfectly good selections of meats, cheeses and organic produce. Still, Maricel would insist on being taken 30 minutes out of the way to a specialty market, and she would ask the store's employees to locate the finest merchandise they had. They would return from the back where they would unearth the most expensive wedge of Gruyere cheese that was cave-aged for 12 months or a Wagyu beef Tomahawk steak, wrapped in brown paper, that they would present to her gently as if they were handing her a newborn baby. She wanted to pay the exorbitant prices; in her mind, the more something cost, the better it was. If the store was out of what she was looking for, she became irate. She would insist the help take her to another more expensive, more out of the way location until she found exactly what she was looking for.

When I first met Maricel, I had the feeling that she was the type of person that could drain the life out of me. Many times before, my first instincts were correct about people but my empathy for her sucked me right in. She tried to get me to pick her up or take her home from her nail appointments by telling me that the last girl who did her nails used to drive her. At first I saw through her cunning ways and I refused, but eventually, she worked it out so that she became my last customer for the day, and she showed up with no ride home. I drove her once because I felt bad for her, and after that, it became a regular thing.

A few times, Maricel's next-door neighbor brought her to get her nails done. I remember Maricel changed her regular appointment to Friday at 3:00 when Judy had her standing blow-dry. It seemed like the ideal situation, but after only a few short weeks, Judy told Maricel she couldn't bring her anymore, and they stopped speaking. I have no idea what happened between them, but I can imagine.

I have to admit I did like Maricel; it was impossible to sit with someone for an hour, week after week, and not grow fond of them. Her accent was heavy, but I was able to understand her perfectly, and we would laugh together during her nail appointments when she recounted stories of her life. I noticed how she manipulated people, but people were also always taking advantage of her.

James was the only person Maricel ever referred to as a true friend of hers, but later I would find out that he borrowed $25,000 from Maricel and never paid her back. James decorated her Christmas tree every year, and he came in handy years later when Maricel needed a date for her son's wedding. James was in his 40s, tall and muscular with a strikingly handsome face. No one suspected at her son's wedding that James was gay, and Maricel loved the attention they were getting. Her ex-husband was there with the woman he cheated on Maricel with and eventually married, and she wanted him to eat his heart out.

Maricel and I made plans to go shopping on a Monday, and I learned that she needed help with absolutely everything because of her vision impairment. She was heavily dependent on me to find the perfect items, and she was extremely picky, but with her money, it wasn't hard for me to find things that she loved. But, before I left to pick her up that morning, my husband took the day off from work. I told him I had plans with Maricel and that I would see him later. I made the mistake of mentioning that Angelo was staying home that day; it seemed to flip a switch in her, and her personality turned from fun-loving to demanding and spoiled.

Maricel was decked out as usual in a pair of skinny jeans, a beautiful blouse with matching jewelry and a pair of Christian Louboutin heels. I also wore heels because they looked better with my outfit, but I knew I would regret doing so because there would be a ton of walking in the shopping mall I was taking her to, with only high-end stores. The smell of her perfume was so strong. She always wore the same perfume. In the salon you could smell her before you actually saw her, but in the small confines of the car the scent was asphyxiating and I was starting to feel sick.

During our 45-minute drive to North Miami Beach, Maricel talked about her son. It wasn't often that she heard from Gus. He had a girlfriend that Maricel always regarded with disgust, and the poor girl didn't stand a chance with Maricel. Maricel would eat her up and spit her out every chance she got. As a result, she hardly saw her son. Gus was picking up a friend at the Fort Lauderdale airport one afternoon. Gus said he would like to stop by to see her on the way to the airport.

"Don't bother if you are only coming for 10 minutes!" Maricel said. As a result, she didn't end up seeing him at all. She was trying to convince me that he was horrible, but I didn't agree with her. I told her what I tell all my clients in this case.

"Maybe if he comes by, and you have a great time together, he will stay longer the next time." I also told her to make his favorite dessert for him so he could bring it home and enjoy it later. I knew how difficult Maricel could be from our conversations over the years, and I was only trying to help, but to no avail, she continued to defend her behavior.

As we entered Nordstrom, we passed the cosmetics and fragrances and as we did Maricel pointed to the perfume she wears.

"You must layer the scent," she said. "First you put on the lotion, then you spray the perfume." That explained the strong odor. We veered to the left and I guided Maricel by her arm. The vast shoe department began to stretch out in front of us. I would love to have perused through the narrow aisles, quietly examining the latest sandals and sneakers, but with Maricel on my heels, I went directly to the smallest display touting only the finest luxury brands. She was not interested in anything less. I held the expensive shoes up one by one close enough for her to see them.

"Do these come in gray?" Maricel asked. "How much are these?"

The salespeople were always extra nice in this section, and a salesman was all over us, but Maricel snubbed him, only wanting me to help her find a pair of shoes, and she finally settled on two pairs to try on. I then handed the salesman the samples.

"She wears a 6 ½." I said.

When he returned, he was balancing five boxes. He was good at what he did, knowing to bring multiple sizes and colors to give Maricel choices. We finally made it out of there with a cumbersome shopping bag containing a pair of grey Chanel pumps for $1200 and a second pair from Alexandre Birman for $650 with a pointy toe in burgundy leather that she could barely walk in.

"Let's put it in my car," I suggested. The car was parked right outside the door, but she would not part with her purchase.

"No, I'm afraid someone will see us and steal them." I knew it was no use, the shoes were coming with us while we shopped, and I was sure I would end up carrying them for her. Just then, my phone rang, and it was Angelo.

"When are you coming home?"

I whispered into the phone. "We just got here, Angelo. It's probably going to be a while." Maricel's whole face changed, and I hung up with Angelo.

"Is he going to keep calling? Now you are going to have to rush, and I am not going to have time to find anything!" I tried to calm her down by telling her how Angelo always calls to check in, that we wouldn't have to rush, but she already was agitated, and there was no reversing it. Walking in and out of the smaller stores, Maricel became increasingly more negative.

"There is nothing for me here, and now I feel rushed!"

I located a few great pieces for her to try on in Tory Burch that she was less than impressed with, and I shoved her into the dressing room. I told her I would be right back, and I went to look for more things while I cleared my head for a second. With a minute to concentrate, I was able to round up a few blouses I knew she would love, all in her size, and I carried them back to the room. She was complaining that nothing was good so far, and she grabbed the new items out of my hands. Before even attempting to try them on, she wanted to know the price of each one, and if it wasn't expensive enough, she scrunched up her face.

"Why is this so cheap?" She handed the less expensive ones back to me.

Over the next two hours, we managed to find a few new high-end items for her wardrobe. It was approaching lunchtime, and Maricel would only go to the best restaurant in the mall that served steak. There were a few places I loved that would have been faster, leaving us more shopping time, but there was only one restaurant that met Maricel's high standards, and it was called The Grille on the Alley. We headed toward the Bloomingdales wing to the restaurant, and as we sat down, she informed the waiter that we didn't want him to rush us under any circumstances. I rolled my eyes and ordered a glass of wine to get through the two-hour lunch, and I swore to myself I would never take her shopping again. I had enough of her already.

Three years later, like going through labor, I must have forgotten the pain.

"I won't go to Gus's wedding if you don't take me to find a dress," Maricel said. "I don't trust anyone else; you are the only one who can help me because you know where to go."

It was true; I did know where to go. I would rather have had one item that I loved than a closet full of ordinary things. Maricel promised lunch at Capital Grille, but I fully intended to pay. Maricel paid the previous time we shopped together.

Gus was getting married in three weeks, so there was no time to waste. I pulled into her driveway at 9:15 the following Monday morning so that we could be in Boca Raton by the time Neiman Marcus opened their doors. I knew from past experiences the day would be all about her, but I could at least see the latest styles.

I had to prepare myself because even if I wanted to browse or buy something for myself, Maricel's demanding requests would dampen my enthusiasm, and I would give up, vowing to try to find the item later online. And this time, I was careful to silence my phone.

I was going to be Maricel's personal shopper for the day and knew I would earn my wings to get into heaven by the end of it. My plan to start upstairs at Neiman Marcus assured complete success. Where were the gowns I had seen over the years walking through the store to the slightly more affordable section? In their place were street clothes right off the runway that were not fancy enough for what we needed. When I questioned her about price and style, Maricel told me that she wanted sparkle of some kind, but she couldn't give me a price range.

"Expensive," she kept saying. "You know what I like."

The only sparkly gown I saw was dreadful, and it had a price tag of $7000. Maricel immediately became nervous, saying we came to the wrong place, but I was sure there must be something else, so I summoned the ancient-looking saleslady. She had been watching us from afar pondering whether or not we were about to waste her time.

We looked like we could spend a ton of money, or at least Maricel did. No one ever knew what to make of us together because of her heavy accent and my perfect English. It was obvoius we were not related. So what was I doing with her? My Gucci loafers and Louis Vuitton bag screamed I wasn't hired help, and I noticed the saleslady's confusion. Sure enough, while Maricel was trying on the $7000 gown, the saleslady whispered to me.

"What's the occasion?" We stood together outside the dressing room door.

"Her son is getting married in three weeks," I said. The elderly saleslady explained how they don't keep the designer gowns in stock, and they must be ordered and sent to the store to try on, but she promised to check the back for anything that recently came in. As soon as she walked away, Maricel scolded me.

"Don't tell them my son is getting married; I don't want anyone to know my business!"

I didn't want to waste any more time in Neiman Marcus. When the women came back empty-handed I told Maricel it was a short walk to Saks Fifth Avenue, and I prayed they had a better selection. All the way there, Maricel went on about how we were never going to find anything, but I promised her I would not take her home without a gown. Up the escalator we went, and as soon as we reached the top, I had a bad feeling. The dresses were much too casual for the mother of the bride, so I looked around for someone to help us before Maricel lost her patience. I found a perky salesgirl dressed in black.

"We are looking for a formal gown for an event next Friday." Then I said a little prayer in my head, Please God, help me find this lady a dress.

It wasn't looking good; there were absolutely no sequins in the entire formal wear section, so I started to go off and search for myself while the salesgirl was trying to talk Maricel into a matronly dress with a few sequins on the bodice. Maricel had an amazing figure for her age, she was a perfect size two, and she deserved better than the tacky dress the girl was holding.

I found a Donna Karan navy gown with ruching at the waist and down the sleeves. It was formal in an edgy way, simple yet elegant, and I knew it would flatter her. They only had two of these gowns, a size two and a size ten. I checked the tag, and the gown cost $2400; I only hoped she didn't find it too cheap. I had to fight her to try it on. She was stuck on sequins, but I promised we would find shoes that glittered. Maricel was reluctant to undress again for what she felt like was a waste of time. She was complaining that there was nothing in these stores and that we should have tried a mall even farther away because someone told her they had a better selection. I had a ton of nervous energy waiting for her to get the dress on already. I began hanging up her outfit while she wrestled with the gown. The private room we were in was large, and there was a pedestal for Maricel to stand on so she could see herself in the three-way mirror. The salesgirl was standing next to me, helping her, and as soon as it was on her body, her whole face lit up.

Except for the length, the gown fit her like it was made for her by Donna Karan herself. The dark blue was so regal on her with her salt and pepper pixie haircut. The slight stretch in the fabric hugged her hips flawlessly, and the dress hung perfectly on her. The salesgirl called in the seamstress and another salesgirl to see Maricel in the dress. The girls were complimenting Maricel on her figure. She was twirling in the mirror, and I knew I had achieved brilliance with this gown.

"We need shoes in a 6 ½, also," I said.

The perky salesgirl's expression was back to business, and she left us in the dressing room while she ran down the escalator to the shoe department. Fifteen minutes later, she was back with three pairs of Jimmy Choo sparkly formal dress heels. The perfect pair was in the first box she opened, and the seamstress was able to pin the dress to the exact length Maricel needed in the back so she wouldn't trip. I asked when the seamstress could have the dress ready, and she said we could pick it up Friday afternoon.

"Impossible, I work Friday," I said.

I knew she could do it right then if we needed her to. I explained how we traveled an hour to get there in the first place, and we needed to take the dress home today. Our salesgirl promised to have it ready in two hours.

Maricel handed me her credit card, and the salesgirl took it to the register. When she brought me the small leather-bound folder for Maricel to sign, I noticed a charge of $140 for the alterations. If you pay $2400 for a dress, you would think the alterations would be free. Saks has hemmed $200 jeans for me for free, but I kept my mouth shut. I wasn't looking for problems. Maricel signed the credit card receipt, and I helped her onto the escalator to go back down.

It was 2:00 by the time we finished there. In four hours, we had accomplished the impossible, but Maricel still insisted we look for a matching handbag on the way out of the store. I didn't see anything that complimented the dress, and I suggested we have lunch because I needed a break.

As soon as we got to Capitol Grille, I ordered a glass of Sauvignon blanc. Maricel ordered her usual steak for $77, and she thoroughly enjoyed it. I'm so glad I treated her because no one ever did, and it was our last shopping trip together.

After we picked up the gown, we walked back through Neiman Marcus to get to the car, and in one of the glass cases we passed was the matching clutch to the Jimmy Choo heels. Bedazzled with silver and rhinestones, it was well worth the $650, and Maricel pulled out her credit card once again to pay. I was exhausted now, but it wasn't over yet.

"I need a strapless bra for the dress," Maricel said. I would rather have had a root canal than to go back up the escalator again, but I helped her up without saying a word.

Her friend James was her date for the wedding. He looked handsome in his tuxedo and Maricel accomplished what she set out to do, looking far better than her ex and the woman he left her for so many years ago, but she was never able to mend the relationship with her son.

The following June, she was out to dinner with a new assisitant. The women she hired brought her husband with her so Maricel would have to pay for both of their dinners. They drove her to the beach to go to a restaurant she loved, but they insisted Maricel pay for the gas because they didn't have enough to get there. Once they sat down, the husband ordered an expensive bottle of wine. During dinner, they were barely paying attention to Maricel, sitting across the table. They were so wrapped up in their private conversation that they supposedly barely noticed when Maricel began to choke on a bite of steak. They continued eating and talking as she slumped down in the booth. By the time the waitress came by and noticed Maricel's lips were blue, it was too late. The manager called an ambulance, and the couple told the police they thought she had fallen asleep.

Judy, Maricel's neighbor, heard the whole story from Maricel's son. Maricel passed away before she got to the hospital. The saddest part was that I may have been the only person who ever missed her.

CHAPTER 6

Ava Molina

AVA MOLINA, A CLIENT OF MINE WAS SEARCHING FOR her birth mother. Reaching into her mailbox, Ava noticed a letter with no return address. Curious, she placed it on top of the stack and walked up the driveway, into the house. Setting the mail down on the counter, she ripped open the envelope and stopped short when she recognized the adoption agency's familiar logo. Ava was 41 years old, her adoptive parents had both passed away and she never expected to hear from the adoption agency again.

Ava's parents never told her she was adopted until she was 21 years old for fear she would feel like she was different from the other children. When they finally told her, Ava contacted the adoption agency hoping for answers. What if her birth mother was out there somewhere worried about her?

The adoption agency tried contacting her birth mother, Marcia, for her, using an address they had on file. Without permission from the birth mother, they could not release any identifying information to Ava. A letter they sent in the mail meant for Marcia, ended up at the house she grew up in, where her mother still lived. Marcia's mother put away the unopened letter until she came to Florida for a visit.

In the meantime, a caseworker from the adoption agency sent Ava a page and a half of non-identifying information. Ava read the pages trying to picture her birth family in her mind. Marcia was 5 feet 3 inches tall, 96 pounds, with brown hair and brown eyes. It was the exact description of Ava. Her birth mother was Italian and Welsh. Maybe that's why people always asked her if she was Italian? There was only a little information about her birth father.

For years, during winter break, Marcia drove down to Florida with her husband and children from Illinois to visit her mother. She was standing in the guest room when her mother handed her the letter. Marcia panicked when she read what the letter said. The adoption agency wanted her to contact them. She shoved the letter into her suitcase and closed the lid.

"What is it?" Marcia's mother asked. She tried to brush it off, saying it was something about an upcoming class reunion.

When Marcia returned to Illinois from the trip, she called the adoption agency. The receptionist connected her to the caseworker who sent the letter. The woman was kind and encouraging. When the caseworker told Marcia her baby's name was Ava, she was shocked. Ava was also Marcia's mother's first name.

Marcia did not want to be contacted again by the agency; she said she put the baby in God's hands when she relinquished her rights. Marcia's mother and her three teenagers never knew about the unwanted pregnancy. Meeting Ava then, Marcia felt, would ruin her life, and her husband agreed.

The caseworker called Ava to deliver the news. She tried to let her down gently, explaining her birth mother's predicament. Ava was newly married and pregnant herself, and she felt her birthmother rejected her twice. Once when she was born, and now again. The non-identifying information would be the only link to her birth mother for the next 20 years. She wondered how her birth mother could be so distant, but she didn't know Marcia's story yet.

At 20 years old, Marcia worked in a travel agency, and she lived in a rented apartment with her best friend, Molly. They both had boyfriends, and one night John, Marcia's boyfriend, had a party at his house when his parents were out of town. Marcia trusted John. He was slightly older than she was, and he met her when he returned home after spending four years in the Navy. He was used to drinking, but there was never any drinking in Marcia's parents' religious home. She hardly remembered the evening after drinking scotch for the first time in her life at the party.

Furious with John when she missed her period, she broke up with him. His mother called Marcia, wanting to help and offered to let her live with them if they wanted to get married, but that was no solution. Marcia's mother would still know she had sex before she was married. Being raised in the church, she felt how dire her predicament was.

If anyone at the travel agency found out she was pregnant, they would ask her to leave. In 1966 women could not work if they were pregnant. Marcia tried not to think about what was happening. She only gained ten pounds, and she wore a girdle and little jackets to hide her growing stomach.

On a rainy night in February, Marcia woke up with sharp pains in her lower abdomen. The sheets felt wet as she tried to get up, and she realized her water broke. She called out for her roommate at the time, Molly.

Molly helped her into the car and drove her to the hospital. The nurses were not very sympathetic when they realized Marcia was unmarried. They told Molly to go home, and Marcia was left alone, frightened, and in pain. She explained to the nurses that she planned to put the baby up for adoption. It may have been her imagination that the nurses regarded her with disgust, but raised in a religious home, they couldn't possibly judge her more harshly than she was judging herself. She was so thankful when they finally administered the anesthesia. Being unconscious during the birth was a blessing. When she woke up, the baby was gone. They never let her see the baby or say goodbye.

A nurse drove Marcia back to her apartment after being released from the hospital. Recovering physically from the ordeal was going to be the easy part. The nurse poured her a glass of scotch before leaving her alone with her thoughts. It was ironic. Scotch was what got her into trouble in the first place.

No one except Molly ever knew Marcia gave up a baby for adoption. When Marcia met the man she eventually married, she confided in him about the baby she gave away, knowing it was the right thing to do. He was sympathetic at the time, and the couple went on to get married and have three children of their own. When Marcia allowed herself to remember her first pregnancy, guilt and shame washed over her. Forgetting it ever happened was the only way for her to function, and there was no time to dwell on the past, given her situation.

Years after the letter arrived at her mother's house, Marcia found out she had stage 2 colon cancer. She received harsh chemotherapy treatments that left her weak and frail. Marcia's husband came into her bedroom and sat down on the edge of her bed.

"Do you want to meet Ava?" he asked. Laying on her deathbed was not how she wanted to be seen by the child she once carried.

"No," Marcia said. "Not like this."

Marcia's husband changed as he got older. He was always verbally abusive to her and the children, but he became violent, and Marcia was afraid of him. When she fully recovered and returned to her job, she finally filed for divorce after 38 years and left the house one afternoon with only a few garbage bags filled with clothes. Marcia's husband thought she was dropping the bags at a donation center. When he realized she wasn't coming back, he called their three children individually and exposed the secret she kept from them for so many years. He may have thought her unwanted pregnancy would turn them all against her, but it did just the opposite. They had empathy for their mother, and they encouraged her to find their sister, Ava.

Marcia told them she didn't know if she could find Ava after so many years, or if Ava would even want to see her after she rejected her in the past. Marcia contacted the adoption agency resulting in the letter sent to Ava's address.

March 1, 2007

Dear Ava,

I work for Children's Home Society, a licensed social service agency, and I am trying to locate Ava Florence Reed, born on February 9, 1966. I have a very important message. The purpose of our contact is to pass along information that is confidential in nature. I am not selling anything, nor am I a bill collector; also, this person is not in any type of trouble. If you are this person, please get in touch with me. Thank you for your assistance.

Sincerely Elizabeth Benson

Caseworker

Immediately Ava picked up the phone to call the number, but it was late Friday afternoon, and the office was closed for the weekend. She would have to wait until Monday morning to get a call back. Ava was praying her birth mother finally wanted to meet her; 41 was the perfect age to be found; all of Ava's dreams of her own family were coming true, she thought, as her husband and children read the letter.

Ava lived with her husband, Andrew, and their two children in a beautiful home. Her son was excited, but her 17-year-old daughter, said she would not want to meet Ava's birth mother if the only grandmother she ever knew was still alive. Timing was everything. Ava's adopted mother passed away recently, four days before her 80th birthday. Ava was by her mother's side in the hospital when she left this earth. She would never want to hurt the mother who raised her, either.

Monday morning, she watched as the clock slowly ticked away. Ava was going to call again at 9:00 but, the phone rang at 8:50. Elizabeth, the caseworker, identified herself and then wanted to be sure she had the right person.

"Did you try to meet your birth mother many years ago, but she didn't want to meet you?"

"Yes," Ava said.

"Well, she does now."

Elizabeth explained the paperwork she needed to be notarized to release Ava's contact information to Marcia. Once the paperwork was received, she could expect to hear from her birth mother in a few days. Ava printed out the forms, had them notarized, and sent them back before going shopping that morning. Later that same evening she was going to dinner for a friend's birthday, and she needed to buy her a gift.

Within hours Ava heard her BlackBerry ring with the familiar sound of an email. Ava was in Bloomingdales, at the register, paying for the gift. When she glanced down at her phone she saw the email was a letter forwarded to her from her birth mother. She was not expecting to hear anything so soon, and she wondered if the salesgirl noticed her hands were shaking as she finished paying. Walking away from the register she looked for a bench where she could sit down to read the email. After so many years of waiting for this day, it was finally here. Ava studied the letter, taking in every detail. She never knew her birth mother's name.

To: Ava Molina

From: Elizabeth Benson

Date: March 5, 2007 11:16:33 EST

Subject: Letter from your birthmother

Dear Ava,

Elizabeth called me this morning to let me know you have a desire to get to know me. I am absolutely thrilled! Please email me; I want to get to know you. I have a son and two daughters. Kurt is 38, and he is married to Patty. They have two boys, Brian and Scott. Melody is 35 and single. We currently live together. Christine is 31, and she and Andy have been married for over six years.

I work as a sales consultant for a publisher, and I have a home office. Please feel free to ask me anything you would like to know about me.

Looking Forward to hearing from you,

Marcia

Ava was terrified to ask any questions for fear of scaring Marcia away, so she cautiously wrote her back, careful not to say the wrong thing. Ava let Marcia know that her life was going well, and she was happily married with two children of her own. A string of emails began that day and continued late into the evening. They were both surprised by how much they resembled each other when they exchanged the first photos.

In 1966, without her mother's support, Marcia had to fend for herself, and she did what she thought was best for the baby. It wasn't easy to hide her pregnancy, but if she lost her job, she wouldn't be able to pay her share of the rent on the apartment, and she would have to go back home. The thought of Marcia's mother finding out about the pregnancy still haunted her. She knew her mother would be extremely disappointed and ashamed of her only daughter. She may even disown her. While Ava couldn't understand Marcia still being afraid of her mother at 62 years old, she accepted that she wouldn't ever meet her grandmother with whom she shared a name. After all, Ava never thought she would meet her birth mother.

In 2006, Marcia moved to Denver, Colorado, to be closer to her children after her divorce, but she still traveled to Florida to visit her mother every year. Marcia said she would love to meet Ava while she was in town that year, but Christmas was over six months away, and Ava couldn't imagine waiting that long after waiting 20 years to meet her.

Ava offered to fly to Denver at the end of the month. She wanted to meet Marcia alone the first time so there wouldn't be any distractions. Her husband worried about her going alone to Colorado to stay with people she never met before, but Ava had gotten to know Marcia pretty well by the time she went. They continued to email every day. And how bad could it be? She was only spending two nights there.

For 20 years, Ava knew her birth mother was out there somewhere. She imagined she would know her if she ever saw her. Ava tried not to have any expectations, but she dreamt of what she would find when she got to Denver. She knew she was overthinking. What kind of first impression would she make? In her small carry-on bag, Ava placed a photo album she made for Marcia to document her entire life. She boarded the plane in jeans and a long-sleeve T-shirt with a matching long sweater, boots, and the Louis Vuitton bag her husband recently bought her as a gift. The only jewelry she wore was her diamond wedding band and a watch.

Ava walked right past Marcia the first time, afraid it wasn't her. There was a gate separating them, and as Ava walked around the side to where Marcia was standing, her birth mother walked over to her. They hugged, and to anyone watching, they must have seemed like any other mother and daughter. Marcia suggested they sit and have lunch before getting into the car to drive to her house.

They both ordered grilled chicken Cesar salads and bottled water to drink. Marcia gave Ava a pair of earrings, and Ava gave Marcia the album. Marcia said when she meets Ava's mother one day in heaven, she will thank her.

As they walked through the airport's parking lot to Marcia's black SUV, Ava asked about her birth father. Marcia had already told Ava his name was John, and she hadn't seen or heard from him since the night she broke up with him. It seemed Marcia was still angry with John by the way she spoke. They made a quick stop to get gas and got back on the road.

Walking into the house, Marcia shared with her oldest daughter; Ava noticed every detail. The house itself felt familiar. Much of the decor was similar to what Ava had in her own home. The house was bright and airy with high ceilings. Melody, Ava's half-sister, was in the kitchen preparing a salad. Marcia planned a dinner that evening, and Ava could smell meatballs cooking on the stove.

Marcia's other children, Kurt and Christine, came over with their families, and everyone sat down at the rustic farm table in the dining room. Ava noticed the ease at which they spoke to one another. She tried to think back, and she couldn't be sure if she ever felt the same comfort with her mother growing up. Ava noticed her upbringing was completely different from her siblings. Marcia and her husband worked for a church, and they lived on church property for years, spending all their time there. Their children were not allowed to watch television or play with Barbies. As they got older, they were forbidden to drink, and sex before marriage was out of the question. Always rebellious, Ava found it fascinating how her siblings obeyed such high demands from their parents.

Marcia never drank alcohol for the 38 years of her marriage, but they all enjoyed a bottle of red wine that evening, and everyone made Ava feel welcome. If her siblings were as shocked by her as she was by them, they didn't show it. They were all so busy talking; Christine's husband had to serve the dinner. When everyone left, Marcia, Melody, and Ava sat up talking late into the evening.

Marcia gave Ava her room, and she slept in a small bed in the guest room. Ava closed the bedroom door behind her, opened up her suitcase, and took out the pajamas she packed, quickly changing and walking into the bathroom to wash her face and brush her teeth. The day was emotional, and she wanted to try to process every minute of it. Pulling back the covers, Ava noticed her birth mother had the same bedding Ava had. She laid down on the soft mattress and covered herself with the fluffy white duvet. She fell asleep within minutes.

The next day, Marcia and Ava walked around downtown Denver and stopped in a little French cafe for lunch, where they ordered several crepes filled with fresh ingredients. Ava described for Marcia what life was like in her house with her husband and children. Most nights she prepared dinner for her family, and she often fed a crowd. The boys in her son's band held practice in the garage in the afternoons, and they loved Ava's cooking. When Ava told Marcia she painted all the walls in her house herself, Marcia thought she sounded very much like John's mother. If Ava could find out her birthfather's last name, her husband could try to locate him on the internet. Finding him was impossible without his full name; they had tried many times. Ava asked Marcia what John's mother's name was, and she said, "I don't remember; I called her Mrs. Carrozza." Ava finally knew her birth fathers name, John Carrozza.

When Ava returned from her trip, she asked her husband to try find John. For some reason, it seemed urgent. It turned out that he still lived in Boca Raton, an hour from where Ava lived with her family. Ava asked her husband to call him.

"John, please"

"This is John"

"Did you know a girl named Marcia, from a while back?

"About 40 years ago."

"Were you aware she was pregnant at the time?"

"Yes. Is it a boy or a girl?"

"It's a girl."

John had cancer, and he didn't know how much time he had left. He wanted to meet the daughter he never knew. Ava wrote to him, enclosing a photo of her daughter and herself at Andrew's recent promotion ceremony. They were both smiling in the picture; they looked friendly and not intimidating.

After receiving the letter, John called Ava, and they made plans to meet and go to lunch. He wasn't feeling well, so Ava said she would pick him up. She knew she could find the house once she got to his street. Her friend, Kim, who was a realtor offered to drive by the house earlier in the week. Ava already had a photo of John's house. He was standing outside, waiting for Ava as she pulled into the driveway. Ava parked her black SUV and walked toward him.

"You sure are a pretty girl," he said.

If Ava saw John on the street, she would never guess this was her birth father. John's hair was already gray, and his skin was tan. But when John motioned for Ava to come inside, she noticed his eyes were clear and blue, just like her daughter's.

The day was bright and sunny outside. Walking into the living room, the air felt chilly, and the room was dark. They sat down in two armchairs at the table, and John showed Ava a picture of his three daughters. Their mother passed away when they were small, and he talked about how he raised the girls by himself. The girls were shocked by Ava appearing out of nowhere, and they had no desire to meet her. Ava understood. After a few minutes they left to go to a restaurant on the water.

They watched the boats go by as they got to know each other. A waitress appeared as John was asking Ava about her childhood. He seemed genuinely curious. The waitress asked if she could bring them something to drink, and John ordered a rum and coke. Ava's drink of choice was always a rum and coke when she was young. That day, she ordered a glass of white wine. She laughed to herself when the waitress returned, thinking about how the waitress might feel if she knew what was happening at the table she was serving. John took a sip of his drink.

"Go ahead," he said. "Tell me what you brought me here to say."

"Did you think I wanted to yell at you?" Ava asked.

John smiled, but she could tell he was bracing himself. Ava assured him she only wanted to meet him and know who her birth father was. John relaxed a little, and he told Ava that his mother was still alive and desperately wanted to meet her.

As Ava drove away from his house, she called Marcia to give her the details. Ava mentioned that John's mother was still alive. Marcia asked Ava for John's phone number. She was ready to speak to him. Ava held her breath while she waited for Marcia to call. The forty-one years since John and Marcia last spoke seemed to vanish during their conversation. When Marcia suggested to John that they all get together for a reunion, Ava wanted to host it at her house.

Marcia flew in from Denver the day before the dinner. Ava picked up everything they needed including flowers and a cake. Nothing was too good for this once-in-a-lifetime reunion. Ava and Marcia left to pick up John and his mother in the afternoon. Ava couldn't wait to meet her paternal grandmother for the first time. She remembered the only grandmother she ever knew fondly. Her adopted father's mother was very soft-spoken and demure. She bought all of Ava's dresses, and they had tea parties together in the afternoon in the dining room. She passed away when Ava was young, and it was hard for her to fathom another grandmother.

Ava's husband prepared steak and lobster tails on the grill while Marcia and Ava prepped the appetizers and side dishes. Before dinner, they all enjoyed cocktails by the pool. John's mother recalled stories of when John and Marcia were dating. For her age, she seemed very modern. The evening was magical for Ava. In her wildest dreams, she never imagined a reunion like this. After dinner, Ava's grandmother said that John was at the doctor that morning and he was in need of a blood transfusion.

"Why didn't you go straight to the hospital?" Ava asked.

"I wouldn't miss this night for the world," John said. He admitted himself to the hospital later that night, and he seemed thrilled when Ava and Marcia came to visit the next day. John told them he needed an operation.

Marcia and Ava were at the hospital on the morning of his surgery. They kissed him goodbye before he was rolled down the hallway, then found a comfortable spot to sit and wait. The surgery took hours, but Marcia and Ava had plenty to say to each other, sitting there for so long. They were still getting to know each other and fill each other in on details of their lives. Marcia described her upbringing and how strict her mother was, but she never talked about the years she was married. It seemed too hard to relive it. Finally, the doctor came out.

"Family of John Carrozza?" Marcia and Ava both stood up and walked over to him.

"Who are you?"

"I am his daughter and this is my mother," Ava said. She felt like a fraud, but she needed information.

"Your father will need to transfer to another hospital. What he needs is more than this hospital can provide."

John was never transferred from the hospital. He passed away early the next morning. Even though it was brief, meeting him in person was a gift Ava is thankful for every day. What if he were already gone when she finally found him? Ava would only have heard about him from other people. She got to meet him, see his mannerisms, and look into his blue eyes. The precious few memories of him Ava will always cherish.

After the funeral, Marcia stayed for a week at Ava's house, working remotely. If John had lived longer, there was a good chance John and Marcia may have ended up together. The love they once had when they were young was still there.

Marcia and Ava spent most of their time alone when Marcia visited. But eventually, everyone in both families joined the happy reunion. For spring break one year, they all went on a family vacation to Salt Lake City. They stayed in two townhomes with warm cozy fireplaces. In the mornings, they enjoyed the views on the snow-covered balconies. It was the perfect backdrop for the families to bond. Perhaps Marcia and Ava were the most pleased; it was a dream come true for them.

For years Marcia and Ava emailed or called each other daily. They had long conversations about life, and although Marcia didn't raise Ava, in some ways, they were very much the same.

One evening at bible study, Marcia met a man named Joe, who recently became a widower. Marcia noticed him once before. Joe was tall with streaks of gray through his thick dark hair. Before the class began, he pulled his chair near hers and sat down.

For weeks during the class, Joe hung on every word Marcia said. Joe asked her for her phone number and started calling her in the evenings. Soon she began to look forward to his calls. Marcia was hesitant to start dating at her age, but she agreed to meet him one night for dinner, and they saw each other every day after that. Having Joe around made Marcia feel young again.

They would never consider living together, so they married in Denver. The ceremony was at the church Marcia attended. Marcia's son, Kurt, walked Marcia down the aisle and gave her away. Afterward, the entire family gathered at the reception. Marcia and Joe chose a ballroom in a nearby hotel for a formal dinner and a night of dancing.

Ava was sensitive to her sibling's feelings and careful not to overshadow the relationships they had with Marcia. New ties are fragile and easily severed. Marcia and Ava's relationship was precious to them. Perhaps no one else could know precisely how they felt. To maintain a relationship with each other that included all the additional family members was not easy. Feeling like they had to prove their loyalty to each family member was exhausting.

Marcia was the one who suffered the pain of her secret being exposed to her children by her ex-husband, and it wasn't his story to tell. Marcia cringed and felt like she was suffocating every time Ava told her adoption story to people. The story sounds like a fairy tale, Cinderella's mother came back for her, unless you are Cinderella's mother. After the wedding, Marcia retired from her job and bought a house with Joe in Alabama. Marcia and Joe no longer want to travel, feeling comfortable to stay put.

While Ava's siblings were busy raising small children, Ava's children have grown, and she has more free time than she has ever had before. Ava and Marcia wrote a memoir for future generations to read their incredible story. When Marcia meets new friends at church, and they asked how many children she has, Marcia said four without hesitation. Ava is just the oldest one who lives in Florida.

CHAPTER 7

Demi Alter

OCCASIONALLY OUR LIVES AND OUR CLIENTS' LIVES intertwined and we became part of each other's stories. Demi Alter's enthusiasm for life won me over but I have to say, I felt a hesitation and a need to be cautious in the beginning, when I first did her nails. That said, I was drawn to her like a moth to a flame.

Maybe it was Demi's blonde hair and slender figure that reminded me of my childhood friend, Paula, or it was the fact that I found her seemingly unending knowledge of how the world works invaluable, and I was hungry to learn. Demi said I was like a little sister to her, and she was willing to teach me everything she knew.

Demi chatted away during her appointments, with her slight southern accent. Her husband, Jason was a successful dentist. Demi's first husband was a jeweler, and she tired of him after a few short years. A friend told her about a single dentist who recently opened his own practice. Demi immediately booked an appointment to see the dentist, and left the jeweler, as a result. I could see how men were attracted to her, she was smart and beautiful; a total package.

The dentist's parents lived in NY, and were thrilled their son finally found someone to marry. They only required her to convert to Judaism before they would plan a wedding. Demi told me that once she learned about Judaism from Jason's rabbi she felt like the religion was something she truly believed in. Jason's parents covered all the wedding expenses and gave them a nice down payment for a house. Demi only had a small settlement from the jeweler, and she had no family to speak of. She talked fondly of her father, who passed away when she was young. Her mother and sisters were evil to her after his death, and Demi hadn't spoken to them in years.

I wondered if people knew how they sounded when they told me stories of themselves. It invariably became clear to me how to interpret what they were saying. If a client told me all three of her grown children weren't speaking to her, I would have to assume there was a reason.

Demi started to describe scenarios in her everyday life that were cause for concern. She screamed at a salesman one day while shopping for her husband in a department store. When Demi paid for a tie with all singles to get rid of the stack she had accumulated, the salesman jokingly implied that the bills were tips and she was a dancer or a waitress. It must have struck a nerve with her.

"How dare you? You probably can't afford to buy one thing in this store!"

"I'm so sorry ma'am. I was only kidding," he said. Demi walked away and the salesman hoped she didn't complain about him to the manager. Women would abandon all self-control in certain situations, telling someone off rather than handling themselves like a lady. When is it desirable for a woman to start screaming at a hairdresser, or a receptionist, or a salesperson? But as I said,

I ignored signs and was only dazzled by her charm when she spoke to me.

Demi invited me to her house to see a rug she wanted to sell. The Karastan rug was too small for her living room, and she had already ordered the larger one. My husband and I had just purchased our first home and I was looking for the perfect rug for our great room.

Hearing about Demi's house while I did her nails every week did not prepare me for how it looked in person. Demi decorated the house entirely by herself, and decorating it with exquisite taste the way she did, was no easy task. It was a mini-castle with billowing damask curtains on every window blocking out the bright Florida sun. All the rooms were lit with antique bronze lamps. Every room was filled with oversized wooden armoires and plush area rugs on top of a mix of oak parquet and travertine floors. The house was on an acre of land and the pool in the backyard was shaped like a four-leaf clover surrounded by enough teak furniture to entertain a crowd of people. The kitchen's ceiling was two stories high and it overlooked a family room with deep brown leather sofas that left an imprint in the cushions when someone sat down.

Demi and the dentist had two boys together. If a child is lucky, they will have at least one emotionally available parent, crucial for their growth and development. Demi turned out to be a sociopath who only had her children as accessories. Demi's boys were perfectly dressed in what were little uniforms. A dozen of the boys' favorite pants, t-shirts, socks, and underwear, perfectly folded in their tiny drawers, were ready to be worn at a moment's notice. She washed and dried all the laundry herself, never wanting help in the house. Demi preferred privacy. She took me upstairs where the boys' rooms looked like they were right out of a magazine. Antique twin beds with fluffy down denim comforters and plaid throws were in each room. Demi bought multiples of everything and stashed them as extras. The rugs in the boys' bedrooms were adorable in the space, but there were at least two spare rugs rolled up under each bed, and dozens of comforters in the linen closet. Demi liked choices. Across the hall was a playroom with all of their toys and a huge television where the boys were watching a movie. Demi asked them to say hello, but mesmerized, their eyes never left the screen.

I listened while she talked about the other mothers she met. "How can they send their children to school with Lunchables in their backpacks?" Demi was not a cook, but she collected perfectly shaped green grapes and baby carrots to go with scoops of tuna and crackers for her children's lunches that she packed in only the finest divided Tupperware free of cancer-causing plastic. I cringed, knowing my daughter was probably eating her favorite Lunchable at that moment.

Whenever her oldest boy played with other children, there was always trouble and it always involved him. A hand would get smashed in the lid of the toy box or a child would get hit in the back of the head with a toy whenever the parents were out of sight. Her son claimed not to know what happened one day when he was alone in a room with a puppy and its leg ended up broken.

After we toured the house we walked into the living room. White upholstered Ralph Lauren sofas sat on either side of the Karastan rug. The expensive rug was meant to be an heirloom, passed down from generation to generation. Framed oil paintings covered one wall and two French chairs sat side by side in the far corner.

"This is the rug." Demi pointed down and slightly to the left. "I love it but it's just not big enough in here." She had already ordered a much larger size so that the sofas could sit on top of the rug instead of around it. The rug was a kaleidoscope of color.

The wool was thick and sturdy and I could understand how after owning a rug of this quality, nothing else could compare. Demi offered to bring the rug to my house once her new one arrived so we could see how it looked.

Angelo and I had been married for a few years at this point. Demi pulled up in the driveway the with the rug sticking out of the back of her Range Rover. Her children were not with her, and I assumed her husband Jason was on daddy duty as he often was. I bought the rug from Demi and when she left, Angelo looked at me.

"Does she cheat on her husband?"

"Why would you say that?"

"Just a feeling," he said.

Angelo was usually right about people. Demi and I started shopping together for more home furnishings. I have always loved to find treasures that needed a little fixing up and turn them into something fabulous. For my son's bedroom I read in a Martha Stewart magazine how to find odd pieces of furniture and refinish each one in the same flat black paint to look like a set.

In a used furniture store I found a solid wood twin-sized headboard and a child's antique desk with ball and claw feet. I sanded and painted the pieces until they looked as smooth as the nails I buffed and polished. I changed out the hardware on the desk to brushed nickel bin pulls from Pottery Barn. I painted the room a soft eggshell color, and added cowboy and Indian bedding to complete the look. When my neighbor came by and saw the room she asked me if I got the furniture from Ethan Allen. I was proud of myself, but Demi never needed to be that resourceful. She didn't work and she could buy whatever she wanted on her Platinum American Express card. She seemed to have it all; a husband who adored her and did whatever she asked, and two little children who were spoiled to the point of rotten.

Jason's parents spent time at their second home in the Hamptons every summer, and Demi and Jason took the boys to visit. Demi didn't take too kindly to her mother-in-law, making a snide comment in front of everyone when Demi added bacon to her plate at brunch.

"Jewish people don't eat bacon." Demi brushed by her mother-in-law and whispered in her ear.

"Fuck you, Sibyl. I've seen you eat bacon when no one is looking."

Her behavior did not fit the wife of a dentist. Still, I was shocked when we met for a drink one day and she told me what she had been up to. Demi had been cheating on her husband for months and she was thinking of leaving him. The guy she was having an affair with told her not to leave her husband; he wasn't looking to get married. He owned a business in the same plaza as the salon I was working in at the time, and he had recently dated one of the other nail techs. He was a confirmed bachelor and definitely a player. I let Demi know he was the devil and to run the other way as fast as she could before he ruined her life. She was not the first bored housewife to cheat but she had more to lose than most.

During the affair, her boys noticed Demi tiptoeing through the house on her cell phone and tried to follow her hushed whispers into the master bedroom. Afraid the young bachelor would hear their little whining voices, she locked her bedroom door and retreated to the back of her enormous walk-in closet. Behind the piles of clothing, she hid while she described the sexual acts she planned to perform the next time she saw him, while the boys were banging on the bedroom door for her to come out.

Demi stopped caring about the house and began shopping for new outfits for herself. Her figure was already slender but she joined the gym and needed all new clothes after a sudden drop in weight. She bought nothing but the best clothing that all the celebrities wore. Instead of admitting to Jason that she was cheating, Demi told him she needed space. She was a lot to handle and a break sounded good to him too. Jason thought she was having a mid-life crisis, the way she was going out every night dressed like a teenager again. He assumed she would get it out of her system eventually so Jason helped her settle into her own place by hanging shelves and art in her new rental. The very next Christmas Demi got a tree and decorated it with Faberge eggs. So much for being Jewish.

There was some extra furniture she wouldn't be needing in the condo. A trunk made of antique pine and a bookcase were two of the one-of-a-kind items. She offered to sell me both pieces and I bought them. She took the best of the best items from the house to decorate her rental. The movers she hired took furniture and curtains and paintings and rugs in their moving truck while Demi had them load delicate antique vases and lamps into her Range Rover with the utmost care, and she drove them herself so none of the precious items would be damaged.

Demi took all the material things she considered to be valuable, but she left her children behind. She claimed she wanted them to grow up in the big house that they were born in. I assume the real reason was she thought she would be more desirable to the young bachelor without her children. By then Demi didn't even want to deal with the little monsters she created. Her two-story cozy rental was closer to the young successful bachelor that she was sure would marry her. As soon as she was settled in Demi had Jason served with divorce papers, so she could receive her settlement. Only a few months later, the bachelor stopped seeing her.

I made the mistake of telling Angelo that Demi was cheating on her husband, like he suspected.

"Why would a young guy want a forty-year-old women with two children when he could easily have two twenty-year-old girls instead?" Angelo had a point.

We had been out to dinner a few times with Demi and her husband, and Angelo felt a loyalty to Jason and threatened to call him about the affair. I begged him not to, and he made me swear I would not be seen with her. Angelo didn't want anyone to get the impression that I was like her.

"Birds of a feather," he said.

I still saw her in the salon, and one morning Demi came in early for her appointment since she wasn't working and had no children to get ready for school. The boys were Jason's responsibility now, she only took them on occasion. My first client of the day, Robin Chess, was still sitting in my chair. Demi wandered over to the makeup counter and began looking at the products. The receptionist let her know if she was interested in purchasing anything, the makeup artist would be arriving any minute. When I was finished with Robin, I called Demi over. When she sat down she had seven or eight lip pencils and an eyeliner sticking out of the pocket of her jean jacket. I assumed those were her choices knowing she never bought just one of anything.

Demi got up to wash her hands and my next client, Joan Schwartz sat down so I could remove her polish. Rotating my clients like this, I was able to fit several more clients per day into my schedule. Having to wash the dust from the acrylic off their hands before I polished their nails, they would go missing for a while. I continued to work on Joan's nails. I could hear what the receptionists were dealing with.

"I can't come in on Tuesday because Phoebe has a piano lesson."

"Wednesday is no good. Sami has a swim meet."

"Can you ask Annie if she will come in early for me on Friday?"

By the time Demi sat back down; the makeup in her jacket pocket was gone. The makeup artist had arrived at this point, and she noticed the items were missing. The receptionist came over to us and asked Demi what she did with the pencils.

"I put them back," she said. She said it so convincingly, even I believed her. It made no sense to me that Demi would need to steal makeup from the salon. She certainly could buy whatever she wanted after the large settlement she received from the divorce. I assumed she would find another husband before it ran out. I had no idea how fast she was spending the money.

I have always been good at networking with my clients, and Demi asked for my help. She wanted to sell her king-sized antique bed and I contacted a client, Tina Shapiro, who I knew would want it. Listening to the stories my clients tell me, I learn so much about each one. Tina was a girl who wanted the best of everything, and she was a little envious of Demi. Although Demi's bank account had dwindled, no one knew it because she still walked around the salon wearing expensive luxury brands. When I told Tina about the exquisite carved antique king-sized bed for sale, Tina had to have it. Demi was very grateful to me for helping her, and she offered me more items for my house if I was interested in any of them. I needed a bigger armoire for our television in our master bedroom, and she had the perfect one. She always charged me less than she originally paid for her things, but it was still very expensive. When I decided to buy the antique armoire I could already picture it in my house. The problem was Angelo. He was working the night shift at the time, and if I bothered him with this he would be annoyed. Angelo would get furious when I moved furniture in the expensive cars he leased for me to drive, so Demi and I planned to move the armoire ourselves one night while Angelo was working. Demi had recently moved again. This time to Fort Lauderdale.

I pulled my Mercedes SUV into her underground parking garage and took the elevator to her loft apartment in the new high rise building. For someone who had no money, she was still living like a doctor's wife. I walked into the vast space, and I could see the view of the downtown buildings, the lights twinkling through the glass door leading to the balcony. The armoire was still in pieces where the movers had left it in the massive living room, so it was easy to load onto a rolling cart the building had for moving large items. Even with my vehicle and Demi's Range Rover it would still take two trips to my house to move the heavy pieces, along with a rug and a few oil paintings she talked me into while we were there.

Luckily, when we got to my house with the first load, my teenage daughter, Teran, was just getting home from a date. I wasn't sure how we were going to move the heavy pieces inside but her date offered to help. Teran was used to my antics; she had been helping me move things her whole life. When we dragged the rolled-up rugs into the house we called them "the dead bodies" because that's what they felt like. Teran's date helped us reconnect the electronic equipment that went inside the armoire so that my husband wouldn't be inconvenienced. As long as he could turn on the television with the remote when he got home there was a good chance he wouldn't even notice the new furniture.

Demi and I left to go get the second load, and when we returned, there was just enough time to put the antique armoire together. I vacuumed the rug and hung one of the oil paintings. I noticed that Demi was eyeing a chair I just had recovered. It was a beautiful chair from the 1940s from Laurie's grandfather's apartment on Miami Beach. Laurie Tepperberg and I had been best friends since first grade and she lived across the street. Laurie would see that I let Demi take the chair, but Demi was relentless when she wanted something, and my easygoing personality was no match for her that night. I believed with my whole heart she was not leaving my house without it. Angelo was on his way home from work and I needed her gone.

"Take it," I said.

The fabric I chose when I recovered the chair matched my living room curtains but how could I deny her anything when she had sold me so many beautiful things for my house that I may not have acquired otherwise?

After Demi left, I locked the door behind her and armed the burglar alarm. Our doors were never left unlocked due to the nature of my husband's job. We lived in a gated community but the gate only provided a false sense of security. If someone really wanted to get in they would find a way. The possibility of a criminal Angelo arrested coming back for revenge was something that kept us diligent about the locks. The public records with our properties information did not include our real names and still don't to this day.

I went into my bathroom to take a shower. The sun was coming up as my head hit the pillow and I heard the front door unlock. My hair was still damp from the shower. I prayed Angelo didn't touch it. He changed out of his uniform and climbed into bed, grabbing my arm and pulling me close before falling asleep within minutes. When Angelo woke up the next day, he asked where all the stuff came from. I replied without making eye contact.

"Demi gave it to me." I loved how it looked in our house. Angelo seemed preoccupied with his own thoughts about work and he never asked again. He was used to things showing up like this, and it wasn't unusual if he came home to a room painted a different color or new curtains on the windows. If I didn't ask permission, he couldn't say no.

I couldn't find my new perfume. I noticed it was missing the night before but I assumed I stashed it under my sink. What made it so obvious that it was gone was that it was the only item on my bathroom counter. We recently renovated the master bath. Two clear sinks that resembled salad bowls sat on top of the vanity with a pale yellow quartz countertop. I am not a fan of things left out for everyone to see. I designed this bathroom to have every available organizing feature, one being a drawer for my blow dryer with an electrical outlet inside, and a recessed wall shelf where the bath towels sat rolled and stacked. Narrow drawers lined either side of the sinks, but the perfume I had left out because of the pretty bottle. Remembering the lip and eye pencil incident I immediately panicked. Why would someone with so much steal from a friend? She obviously had a problem.

Then Demi's behavior seemed like she was either mentally ill or on drugs. She became paranoid. She was convinced that people were coming into her apartment while she was out and moving things around. I had never seen someone change so drastically in such a short amount of time. Many times women lost their confidence and transformed into a completely different person after a bad break-up. Women who were getting divorced often dressed differently and seemed to take on a new personality, but Demi was hardly recognizable as the expert on life she once was.

Getting more and more desperate, Demi told me stories about the guys she was meeting online. In six years, the settlement she received in the divorce was almost completely gone, and she needed to sell more of her things. Instead of admitting she blew the money, Demi was telling people someone stole her identity, and her bank account was depleted. She changed her name on social media, and even tried to get her ex-husband back at one point. Jason had not remarried either, but he told her if he saw her bleeding on the side of the road he wouldn't stop to help her. The other moms Demi had once been friends with avoided her phone calls, and gossiped to Jason about her bizarre behavior.

The next time I saw Demi she had a new plan. She made an appointment with an attorney to see if she could get a portion of Jason's inheritance. She was positive she could get it; meanwhile Jason's parents were still alive and well in New York and they had no intention of letting her have a penny.

The younger son still spent the weekends with Demi now and then but the older one would not. She brought the younger son in to the salon with her. He was sweet when she mentioned the mysterious people who were coming into her house, and tried to stick up for her.

"Someone moved the books on the shelf, didn't they?" Demi asked him.

"Yes," her son said, "they turned them like this." He pushed a nail buffer that was sitting in my desk over about a centimeter.

Demi only occasionally came to the salon after that, and each time she did she had a new job or opportunity to make money. But there was always a red flag. She worked for a dermatologist who she claimed gave her some expired Botox. She was looking for someone to inject it into her face. Did she not think I would know she stole it? Demi was eventually fired from the dermatologist's office.

When the lease was up on her condo, Demi moved everything she had left into an air-conditioned storage unit. She wanted to return my chair, no longer needing it since she had nowhere to live. I met her at a gas station next to the building of storage units, and I followed her onto the property. After she pressed the code into the small pad that opened the gate, we parked. Again, I had the same uncomfortable feeling I always had around Demi. Once we were alone in the storage unit I looked around. She had a sofa in the middle of the space that she may have been sleeping on. Her hair that was once blown dry twice a week looked like straw and there was a box of clothing that she possibly fished through each day to get dressed. No longer was she showing off her tiny frame in designer jeans and heels. Instead she had on khaki knee-length shorts and a pair of hiking sneakers that hid the fact that she needed a pedicure.

I felt so bad for her that I ended up buying another oil painting she had propped up near the chair and we loaded the two items into my SUV. I wrote her a check for the painting and she asked me for a favor.

"Can you put my storage unit in your name? I am three months behind on the payment, but you can have everything inside." I stood there not knowing what to say.

"I just need you to pay the rent until you empty it." There was a ton of valuable things in the unit, but I would never get involved in whatever was going on.

Demi's oldest son went away to a college. He no longer had to be the boy whose mother left him; he had a chance to be whoever he wanted to be. Playing video games in his dorm room with friends, the last thing he expected was for his mother to knock on the door. When he saw her he looked at her with horror. Demi was hoping to stay with him for a while. He stepped out into the hallway and shut the door so his friends wouldn't hear him.

"Get the fuck out of here, Mom!"

Another client texted me a screenshot of Demi's mugshot. She moved to California to work for a man she met online. The man let Demi live in his guest house and she was arrested for embezzling money from him. The boys begged their father to bail her out of jail, after all it was still their mother. Jason reluctantly got her out of jail, and no one has heard from her since.

CHAPTER 8

Simone Seigel

WHENEVER MY DAUGHTER OR ONE OF MY FRIENDS
moved to a new house, organizing the closet was my job. An
empty closet was like a blank canvas; the clothing, shoes, and bags
were the art. The wardrobe, when finished, was pleasing to the
eye and also functional. The shelves were like a puzzle with each
item fitting into its designated spot, making them easy to locate.
Nothing is more annoying than searching half-dressed for the
black sweater buried under piles of discarded items.

Slim velvet hangers take up less space than bulkier wooden
or plastic ones, and most of us needed all the closet real estate we
could get. The amount of velvet hangers required to do the job
was usually a shock. Why don't we let go of what we aren't wearing? People only wear ten percent of the clothing hanging in their
closet most of the time. A dress worn on an unforgettable evening
should not be a souvenir.

If I only had to empty the closet, organize the clothing, and
put it all away, the job would be simple. More often than not, every
single item had to be taken off the hanger and tried before being

placed into one of the three designated piles. It should be simple: yes, no, or a maybe. The maybe pile was saved for last and revisited at the end. It's easier to discard a black blouse once you see ten similar tops hanging in the closet already.

Five hours is the time it takes to organize the average woman's closet completely. After talking about organizing closets at work, some clients became interested in my services. If I were to create a business out of it, I needed to set a price per hour, and I started at $50.

A new way to make money seemed fun and exciting. My children were more independent, and my mom-duties were becoming nonexistent. Afraid of being one of those moms that clung to their children a little too long and had no life of their own, I felt the need to keep evolving. I dreamt of ways to help people sort their things. Taking the discarded items with me to drop off at a donation center could prevent the client from pilfering through them later. I filled my trunk with various-sized boxes for storage. Packing away clothes that didn't fit allowed more space in the closet for the currently wearable items.

My client Simone Siegel's closet was one of my first paid organizing jobs. I drove to her house on a Saturday morning, ready to work. I planned to be there for five hours, give or take. Simone was an acquired taste. It was challenging to fill the nail appointment after hers because she often offended people. Never having anything nice to say about another woman, she only criticized how they looked, raised their children, or spent their money.

Simone and her husband lived in a two-story modern contemporary style house with a pool and tennis courts, built in the 80s, on a large property in Southwest Ranches. I parked my car at the end of the drive near the street so I wouldn't be in anyone's way. The garage door was open. I walked inside and knocked softly on the door leading to the house. The cleaning girl came out, leaving for the weekend, and Simone ushered me inside. We stood in the kitchen for a moment while Simone's husband Lee finished getting dressed in the master bedroom.

"Lee woke up late," Simone said, "I already brought him his towel."

Simone was late to her nail appointment once because Lee was taking a shower. Lee only would dry himself with a warm towel. He insisted Simone throw a towel in the dryer for him while he showered. They had one son Ethan who was doing homework in front of the television in the great room next to us.

"Ethan, can you say hello to Annie?"

"Mom, can you be quiet? I'm trying to study," Ethan said, annoyed.

"It's ok," I said. Simone lowered her voice for Ethan, and we walked into the living room. I remember Simone spoiling Ethan as a child. She would pick up sushi and deliver it to the front office at his school right before lunch break. She seemed unaware that she was doing anything out of the ordinary, and now she wondered why he was so foul.

Simone's house had built-in custom waterfall mica furniture in every room. The most significant piece was two stories high and held the flat screen television. Every surface was some version of white or beige except for the colorful contemporary art that hung on every wall. The house was immaculate even if the style was slightly dated. Lee finally came out, dressed for the gym. Simone and I walked into the bedroom.

The closet was not as big as I expected it to be, but then I realized there were two master closets, and Simone's was the smaller one. Lee's shoes were on pull-out shelves in his closet, and a valet sat where he hung his suit for the next day with a short shelf for his watch and wallet. His hangers looked like someone used a tape measure to space them apart. Lee didn't need my services. Shelves wrapped the length of Simone's less-neat closet for her shoes and bags. There was space for long and short hanging clothes, and a row of narrow drawers that locked for her jewelry and sunglasses. She had items she wore less often in the front of the closet, and she had to reach far into the back for things she wore every day. I needed to switch out her hangers and remove what she was no longer wearing.

Simone was a perfect size 8, but she had size 6 and even some size 4 mixed in. She bought the smaller items when she was dieting, but she could no longer get them over her hips. The first thing I did was wrap them in acid-free paper and pack them in boxes. Simone took them to a spare room and put them in a closet that no one used. Then she began the painful process of trying on her clothes one piece at a time. Alice and Olivia tank tops, Theory blazers, Ted Baker blouses, followed by an array of designer jeans, Trina Turk dresses, and jumpsuits. One by one, I hung the ones we were keeping on brand new hangers, tossing the dry cleaning hangers to the side.

"The cleaning girl is supposed to switch out my hangers," Simone said. The cleaning girl is too busy in Lee's closet, I thought.

While I worked, Simone tried things on and talked to me, and before long, I was ready to move on to the dress pants. Half whispering, Simone leaned into the closet and told me she hadn't slept in this room in ten years because her husband snores. Many of my clients had this issue. When she asked me if my husband ever tries to have sex with me, I tried not to answer her personal question and change the subject instead. It's a tactic I use in the salon all the time.

"Do you think you will ever wear these low-waisted pants again?" I asked.

"I can't remember the last time Lee and I had sex," Simone continued.

Luckily, Ethan began yelling for Simone, and she left the room. I had all the pants on new hangers, and I began organizing them by color. I decided not to hang the jeans; there were two empty shelves perfect for folding them, and it freed up more space on the rods. I stacked the jeans on the shelves, and arranged them from dark to light. Simone could pull one out without disturbing the stack.

"Ethan needed me to make him a cappuccino," Simone said. She walked back into the closet. "I love what you did with the jeans," Simone said, glancing at the shelves. "It looks like a boutique."

"That's the idea," I said.

Simone's cleaning girl would get the three large black trash bags full of clothes we eliminated. She was about to be the best-dressed cleaning girl ever. Simone's shoes, still in their boxes, were piled high. I preferred to store them this way, so they never accumulated dust. I organized the boxes by brand, Gucci, Ferragamo, Jimmy Choo, and Stuart Weitzman and then grouped them by style before wiping down the adjustable narrow wood shelves and returning them with the stickers on the boxes facing out. Each tag had a description of the shoe. The top shelf I saved for Simone's designer bags. None of them were in the dust covers that came with the bags. I stuffed them with tissue and faced them forward so she could see them at a glance. Somewhere in the distance, we heard a door slam. Ethan left without saying goodbye. When I finished, Simone complained that $50 an hour was too much. Her cleaning girl only got $17. I told her to pay me whatever she wanted. She paid me $25 per hour. The money I made was far less than I would have made in the salon. It made me appreciate being a nail tech even more. I'm glad I never quit my day job.

Ethan found someone to marry him in his last year of college. What girl would put up with his entitled attitude, I wondered?

Her name was Margaret. They were very similar. Margaret studied abroad for a year in high school like Ethan did, and they both spent summers at the same sleep away camp. They met on a Birthright trip to Israel.

Simone brought Margaret to the salon to have her nails done soon after the engagement. I shuddered to think about what kind of mother-in-law Simone would be. Always critical of everyone, I assumed she would give her new daughter-in-law a hard time, but Margaret was not intimidated by Simone. Margaret never got along with her mother, and she had no intention of bowing down to Ethan's. Like all the young girls today, she could care less if her mother-in-law liked her or not. I watched as they struggled to get along. Finally, Simone conceded control, knowing she would never win. Margaret was a beautiful girl, and she made Ethan happy. The young couple was determined to make all of their own decisions, yet they didn't mind the parents paying for the wedding where they received enough money for a down payment on their first home.

Margaret was in fierce competition with her friends, just like Simone always was. She wanted a diamond eternity band for Ethan to place on her finger at the wedding ceremony. Margaret's friends all had diamond eternity bands when they got married. It started to annoy Simone that Margaret put so much pressure on her son. The diamond band could have been an anniversary gift ten years or even five years later. Simone's band was plain gold, and there was no way she would allow her daughter-in-law to outdo her. Ethan needed help paying for the band, and the family jeweler was thrilled when Ethan and Simone walked into his store. Simone and all of her friends had practically paid for the jeweler's second home with their purchases. Ethan pointed out the ring that Margaret so desperately wanted. Round stones in a white gold setting wrapped entirely around the band. Simone asked to see an eternity band in the display with emerald-cut stones more substantial than Margaret's, every single one a perfect transparent rectangle. It fit Simone's finger perfectly, and she wrote a check for both rings.

At the salon the day before the wedding, Simone bragged to everyone about the wedding band her son bought Margaret while I did the whole wedding party's nails—all the bridesmaids, the bride, and even Simone's mother. Simone's mother, Myrna, was like a second mother to Ethan. Simone never needed to hire a babysitter for Ethan; Myrna was always ready and willing to watch him.

After the wedding, I continued to do Margaret's nails. There were often two types of girls. One knew what she wanted but had no money, and the other had money but no idea what to do with it. Margaret was the latter. Until one of her friends bought something, Margaret wasn't aware that she needed it, but once she figured things out, not only did she copy her friends, she one-upped them.

Shopping became a full-time job for Margaret. Never on impulse, she painstakingly researched everything she bought. Margaret asked everyone in the salon what the best items were to purchase, and she let them influence her every thought. Interestingly, she snubbed some of the salon clients who had the most money but didn't flaunt it and then bowed down to women who looked rich. What a difference there was between old money and new.

Margaret was bothered to the core if anyone acquired something better than she had or had something before she did. She prided herself on knowing what the next "It" bag was, and she wanted to be the first one to carry it. After becoming friendly with the salespeople in her favorite stores, they would contact her when rare- hard to find items came in. Her friends wondered how she always seemed to have the best of the best.

The latest SUV with a rare interior color- check.

Vacation on a sold-out cruise- check.

The largest house in the neighborhood- check.

Margaret's friends began to notice how she spent money, and they envied how Ethan never gave her a limit, replenishing her checking account whenever it was low.

Simone and Margaret both had their nails done on Friday afternoons. Long after I finished Simone's nails, she would hang around the salon. She was paying for both of their manicures while Margaret was still in my chair. Our conversation was about Margaret's new decorator. With the designer's help, she was picking out new rugs and chairs and window treatments.

"Whatever you do, don't tell Simone who my decorator is; she's dying to know," Margaret said. When Simone walked back toward us, Margaret stopped talking.

Right out of college, a large investment group hired Ethan as an advisor. Simone and her husband moved all their money into an account so Ethan could manage it, and they were impressed by the returns they were receiving. Other family members began to invest, and Simone guessed that Margaret was spending Ethan's money as fast as he earned it.

Margaret started to act like she was better than everyone else. She brought an article from a local news magazine about police cars parked overnight in our neighborhoods' driveways.

"Have you seen this?" Margaret asked. Among the many restrictions, our city did not allow parking of open bed trucks or cars with writing on them, claiming they were an eyesore. The article said the police cars in the driveways made the neighborhood look like a trailer park. Margaret agreed with the article even though she knew my husband worked in law enforcement, and he sometimes drove a marked police car. I practiced my self-control, and never let her know what I was thinking.

After two years of marriage, Margaret posted she was 13 weeks pregnant on social media. Simone was furious her son didn't tell her before they announced it to the rest of the world. Everything about the pregnancy was secretive, including the sex of the baby, and I asked Margaret if she decided on a name.

"We have, but we aren't telling anyone what it is."

Only Ethan was in the delivery room when the baby was born. The rest of the family sat in the hospital's waiting area.

Margaret and Ethan were very protective of the new baby girl they named Mila. When the doctor told Margaret she could go back to the gym, she allowed Simone to care for Mila for a few hours in the mornings three days a week to work out with a trainer and do a little shopping. Margaret left strict instructions; under no circumstances was Simone allowed to drive the baby anywhere.

"Who the fuck do they think drove Ethan around his whole life?" Simone asked me.

"They will get over it when they have a second baby," I told her.

While Simone was at their house babysitting, she carried little Mila outside for some fresh air and noticed new patio furniture by the pool. Everything Ethan and Margaret owned was ultra-modern. Simone turned over the cushion to see who made the lounge chairs. She planned to stop at the patio furniture store where she had always been a customer on the way home. The store carried the brand, and Simone ordered the set for her house. She was shocked by the price. It was $10,000 when all was said and done. Furious that Simone copied her, Margaret asked me what she should do about it.

"Imitation is the sincerest form of flattery," I said. I hoped to diffuse her anger.

By the time Margaret was pregnant with their second child, a boy, the entire house had gone through a renovation, changing the porcelain floors to marble and the carpeting in the bedrooms upstairs to wood. All the lighting was new, and so was most of the furniture. The 6-foot tall giraffe stayed in the neutral-colored nursery, and Mila moved to a big girl room of her own with pink walls and a plush white area rug. The new baby boy wasn't due for ten weeks when Margaret started having labor pains. Ethan called his mother to come over so he could rush his wife to the hospital. The doctor prescribed medication and complete bed rest for the remainder of the pregnancy. Margaret's mother was too busy to help, but Simone spent every day at Margaret's house taking care of Mila. The little girl dragged her grandmother to see her new bedroom. It appeared to be straight out of the Restoration Hardware catalog.

"When did you do all this?" Simone asked.

"We ordered the furniture months ago," Margaret said. Simone assumed Margaret's parents must be helping them. It turned out the furniture was ordered from the Restoration Hardware catalog. Money was flowing through their house like water.

The new baby boy arrived a week before his due date, and the baby nurse returned. Two babies were going to be even more work than one. There was laundry to do and bottles to make. Ethan had to pick up dinners every night from various restaurants if he wanted to eat dinner, but then again, Margaret had never been a cook.

Once Margaret was feeling more like herself, she hired a live-in nanny. With her days free, Margaret was able to start shopping again. She was always the best dressed at every event, and so we're her children. In Pilates class, Margaret and her friends wore designer yoga pants and matching sports bras.

A few of the girls in Pilates had recently had a Mommy Makeover by a top plastic surgeon in the area. The Mommy Makeover was a cute name for breast implants and a tummy tuck. Margaret booked a consultation with the doctor. The doctor's office took up the entire second floor of the medical building. He saw patients on one side, and his surgical center was on the other. Feeling nervous, Margaret sat in the opulent waiting area to fill out the required paperwork. Finally, a nurse called her back and handed her a gown.

"Panties can stay on," the nurse said. Then she left the room.

Margaret removed her shoes and clothes, folded them carefully, and laid them on the chair. An album of before and after photos sat on the counter, and Margaret scanned the pages. She felt excited that her body could look even better than before she had the babies. When the doctor entered the tiny examining room, the scent of rubbing alcohol hung in the air as the doctor closed the door. The nurse returned to the room while the doctor explained the procedure.

Before Margaret left the office that day, she booked her surgery for the following month, and she knew she would need help with the children; she wouldn't be able to lift anything for weeks. Her mother lived in Naples, only an hour and a half away, but rarely saw Margaret or her children. Divorced from Margaret's father for years, her social calendar was full in Naples, and she didn't like to travel.

Simone helped Ethan care for the children while Margaret recovered from the surgery. When she took Margaret to the doctor to remove her stitches and they saw the results, Simone booked an appointment with the doctor. Margaret thought it was ridiculous for Simone to have the surgery at her age. Did she have to do everything Margaret did?

At one point, all of Margaret's friends were taking off their acrylic nails and getting gel polish instead. I soaked off her acrylics and gave her a gel manicure, as she requested. Margaret paid $35 and gave me her usual $10 tip. When Margaret came in for her next appointment, her polish had chipped on a few nails. She asked me to do it over for free. I hated the money part of the job, it was so awkward, but I charged her. I explained that gel polish was not as strong as acrylic, and as her nails grew out from the acrylic, the gel would last longer. Margaret reluctantly paid me for a full set of acrylic, and she continued to get her nails done with me, but she only tipped me $5 from that point on.

For Mila's fifth birthday, Margaret planned a party for her, and it was going to be a big one; it was her last year in preschool. Margaret enrolled her in a private school for kindergarten in the fall. It would be the last time she would be with all her little friends, most of them getting ready to attend public school.

"Does Mila need to go to private school?" Ethan asked. He knew that Margaret would want their three-year-old son to go to private school one day too. The tuition each year for each child would cost the same as a semester of college. Margaret was annoyed. How dare Ethan question her decisions when he was always too busy working to help her?

Ethan went to see his Grandmother Myrna unexpectedly one day. He drove up to her house, memories flooding his head. He spent so much time there when he was small, exploring the expansive backyard and wandering through the pine trees at the back of the property when his grandfather was still alive. The house looked the same; Myrna never changed anything; she only maintained it. Ethan rang the doorbell. When Myrna saw Ethan, she was shocked.

"Is everything all right, sweetheart? Are you by yourself?"

"Yes, Grandmother, everything is fine."

Myrna stepped aside so Ethan could enter the foyer. The house smelled familiar to Ethan. It was a mix of the musty antique furniture and the Hermès perfume Myrna was wearing that Margaret bought her for her 75th birthday. Myrna was not anything like her daughter Simone. She spent money on classic designer clothes, and she kept them for years. The blouses she wore with her polyester pants were so delicate they reminded Ethan of tissue paper. Her size never changed, and she still had a beautiful figure for her age. She was wearing the only jewelry she ever wore; a Cartier watch and a bracelet on the same hand as her plain wedding band.

"Are you hungry?" Myrna asked.

"Thirsty," Ethan said. He followed his grandmother into the kitchen. The kitchen was bright and sunny and overlooked the orange and grapefruit trees in the backyard.

"How are the babies? And Margaret?"

"Fine."

Myrna poured Ethan a glass of iced tea, and they sat down at the table. Ethan had eaten many meals at the sturdy table made of antique pine when he was younger. Simone and Lee would go away on vacation when Ethan was small and leave him with his grandparents for weeks.

"I'm here about an investment, Grandma." Myrna smiled, and the corners of her eyes creased. She loved Ethan so much, and it was good to see him.

"You have all my money already," Myrna said. "I trust you. Invest it however you want."

"This is separate from the other investments," Ethan explained. "It's paying a higher return rate, and I have a chance to make you some real money quickly." Ethan knew Myrna had a money market checking account.

"I have the money market account," Myrna said. She walked over to her desk and pulled the checkbook out of the drawer.

"How much is in there, Grandma?" Ethan asked.

"I think a little over $350,000. How much should I write it for?"

"All of it, I will have it back to you in no time." Ethan stayed a little while changing lightbulbs in the recessed lighting that had burned out. When Ethan said it was time for him to get back to the office, Myrna walked Ethan to the door.

"Give my love to your family, Ethan."

"I will, Grandma."

Ethan kissed her on the top of her head.

Ethan used Myrna's money to pay off credit cards that he maxed out. Margaret was not aware of the balance on the cards; she thought her husband was very successful, and Ethan wanted to keep it that way. Simone found out that Ethan used the funds when Simone's brother needed to borrow money, and Ethan couldn't come up with it. Ethan tried to talk his way out of it, but Simone was furious, and she called Margaret and told her that Ethan stole Myrna's money. Margaret refused to believe Simone. After all, what would she do if it were true?

Myrna begged Simone to forgive Ethan; it was not worth losing a child over, but Simone was furious, thinking how Ethan had helped himself to a portion of the future inheritance that should have been hers. Simone never spoke to her son or his family again, but she showed me posts of them from social media during her manicures.

CHAPTER 9

Julianne Portman

JULIANNE PORTMAN WAS RUNNING LATE TO HER 2:00 appointment to have her hair done. She was naturally blonde but adding a few highlights around her face brightened up the color even more and made her fair skin glow. When Julianne arrived at the salon, her hairdresser was still working on someone, so the receptionist offered her a coffee. The coffee smelled delicious, and Julianne realized she hadn't eaten anything all day.

The salon always served refreshments, and there was a tray of bagels next to the coffee. Julianne spread a tiny bit of cream cheese on one-quarter of a sesame bagel and sat down to wait. Carbs were not on her diet, but the bagel was so fresh; she couldn't resist. As she swallowed the first bite, something in her throat felt strange.

It wasn't the first time. For a few days, Julianne noticed something off when she swallowed. She dug her cell phone out of her bag and texted her sister. Her sister was married to a gastroenterologist. If anyone would know if she should be concerned, it was him. As she threw her phone back into her bag, one of the shampoo area assistants appeared with a robe and led her to the shampoo bowls.

By the time Julianne left the salon, she had three texts, and two missed calls from her sister. They lost their mother to Melanoma when Julianne was only a year old. Cancer was always at the back of their minds.

Julianne's brother-in-law was on staff at the hospital, and when he got the call from his wife, he made arrangements for someone to take a look at Julianne. She was planning to go home right after her hair appointment, but she headed over to the hospital. While she drove with one hand, she touched the outside of her neck to see if she could feel anything unusual. Maybe it's nothing, she thought, but better to check it out.

Julianne's twin 14-year-old daughters, Amber and Stella, were on their way home from school. Julianne called Amber, but she didn't pick up. It was the girl's first year of high school. They were very trustworthy, and she knew they would get a snack and start their homework even if she wasn't there.

The doctors ran tests and discovered that Julianne had lymphoma. Her chances of survival were good, but she needed five rounds of chemo. For one week each month, she had to remain in the hospital. The chemotherapy was administered through an IV. The doctors admitted Julianne to the hospital to begin the first treatment.

Julianne dreaded calling her ex-husband, Allan, but she needed him to pick up the twins. Just as she suspected, he was horrible to her. He even accused her of lying about the diagnosis. Finally, he said he would pick up the girls for the week. Julianne called Stella and Amber and told them there was no reason to worry; she would be back home soon.

The first treatment was scary for Julianne, not knowing what to expect. When she felt a little nauseous, the nurses quickly gave her an anti-nausea drug into her IV. She had a private room all to herself, and the nurses were wonderful to her.

Rachel Sachs, one of Julianne's friends, went to her house and packed up everything she needed for the week and drove over to the hospital. Rachel and Julianne had become close after Rachel's divorce. They often went out together on the weekends when the twins spent time with Allan. There were still places for singles to meet, but online dating became the most convenient way to find someone.

Julianne preferred first dates over a committed relationship. She happened to be dating a nice guy named Larry, and he came to visit her in the evenings at the hospital. Larry was walking into her room as Rachel finished unpacking Julianne's things. They all watched a movie together, and Rachel quietly left after Julianne and Larry fell asleep.

When all of Julianne's beautiful blonde hair started coming out in clumps, she used an electric trimmer to finish what the chemo started. After her first treatment, she spent lots of time with her girls. They started collecting designer scarves and wigs for Julianne to wear when she finally went out.

I did Julianne's nails for years, and she was the only girl I knew who could break up with a guy and find a new one while entirely bald. Rachel picked Julianne up one night to go to happy hour. With her new wig, she looked as pretty as ever, and she was excited for a night out.

Russell was at the bar when they arrived. Julianne dated him in the past. He was a great guy and Julianne always compared all her dates to him. He set the bar high. While they were dating they were getting along fine, but then he broke things off so he could give his marriage another try. When she saw him sitting at the bar, she assumed his marriage was over for good.

Russell walked over to Julianne and kissed her on the mouth. He said he thought about Julianne all the time and missed her terribly. They talked about her diagnosis and treatment over cocktails. At one point, she lifted her wig to give him a glimpse of her bald head.

After an hour of talking to strangers, Rachel finally left Russell and Julianne at the bar. They were so engrossed in their conversation; they hardly noticed she was gone. Russell brought Julianne back to his house, where they spent the night together. Cancer made Julianne a little less concerned with other people's feelings. She broke up with her boyfriend, Larry, on a text the next day and started seeing Russell again.

For the second round of treatments, Julianne was better prepared than she was the first time. She packed a rolling suitcase for her week's stay at the hospital as if she was going to the Ritz-Carlton. No more hospital gowns, for Julianne, she had new loungewear and matching socks. When Russell showed up at the hospital to spend time with Julianne, the nurses were impressed with her new boyfriend.

Julianne never looked the slightest bit sick, except that she had no hair underneath the designer scarf on her head. For one hour each day, while the nurses changed her sheets, Julianne was unhooked from the IV. She showered, reapplied her sparkly eyeshadow and lip gloss, and sprayed herself with flowery clean scented body spray.

In the afternoons, Julianne's hospital room swarmed with her sisters and her friends. Instead of meeting at a swanky little spot for lunch like they did before, they would bring in food from a restaurant to the hospital room. Rachel was designated to pick up lunch one day, and she arrived with three pizzas, a salad, and garlic rolls.

Rachel entered the hospital's west wing and took the elevator to the fourth floor, where the patients received life-saving chemotherapy treatments. Washing her hands in the sinks provided in the hallway, she could already hear chatter inside the private room where the festivities were going on before she reached the door's handle. Trays of food covered the countertops along the wall, everyone contributing to a pile of cookies and candy, licorice, and every flavor of popcorn.

I was sitting at the foot of Julianne's bed, painting her nails, when Rachel walked in. The rolling tray table that held a Kleenex box and a pitcher of water became a makeshift manicure table. Julianne was an inspiration for anyone going through cancer treatments. Her attitude remained positive throughout the whole ordeal.

Although her ex-husband Allan cared for the girls during Julianne's stints in the hospital, Allan and Julianne weren't getting along. Like most divorces, their divorce was stressful and was the last thing she needed for a full recovery.

By fall, Julianne was finished with her treatments and Russell had started talking to his ex-wife again. Julianne updated her profile on all the dating sites and sat back as the guys lined up to meet her.

Meanwhile, Julianne and Russell had previously made plans to take her girls to Disney World for the weekend. Rachel offered to go instead since Russell was out of the picture, and they made it a girls' trip. Rachel's son was in college in Orlando, and she hoped to see him at some point. It was a three-hour drive, and they decided to take Rachel's car, a Mercedes her ex-husband bought her while they were married. The four of them piled into the comfy seats wrapped tightly in leather. The girls were just back from their father's house, and they were excited to tell Julianne and Rachel about his new condo on the beach. Allan had been renting an apartment since the divorce, and finally, he bought a place. It was small, but it sat right on the sand, and it had a roof-top patio above the two-car garage. The girls loved staying on the beach.

Disney World was packed, but the weather was cooler than usual. Rachel and Julianne walked around while the girls rode all the rides. The second day was warmer, and the girls were happy to lay out by the pool instead of returning to the park. Rachel's son joined them. Stella and Amber had so much fun with him. He treated them like two little sisters, tossing them into the air and watching them land in the water.

Rachel and Julianne had a falling out on the phone a few weeks later. Stella told her mother that Rachel's son offered her a pot brownie after their swim. When Julianne called Rachel to confront her, it started a war. Rachel accused Stella of lying.

"Why would Stella lie?" Julianne asked.

"Your girls aren't as innocent as you think!" Rachel said.

Julianne hung up the phone. Weeks later, Julianne and Rachel still were not speaking. Rachel wanted to forget the whole thing, but Julianne would not. She never wanted to be friends again. And if any of her friend groups got together with Rachel; Julianne refused to go.

One afternoon, while at work, Rachel got a text from Tom, a guy that was always texting her. They made plans to see each other that evening. After work, Rachel threw on a new outfit; she looked great, but she wasn't excited to go. She had been out with this guy before, and he was more interested in her than she was in him, but Rachel accepted the invitation; it was better than doing nothing. Rachel never thought she would be single for this long when she divorced her husband. Where was her Prince Charming? When Tom picked up Rachel, he asked where she would like to go, and she suggested JAlexander's. At least the food and drinks were good, she thought. The bar at JAlexander's was a favorite spot for all the singles in Plantation.

Rachel walked in front of Tom as the hostess led them to a table. As she sat down, Rachel glanced around and spotted Allan, Julianne's ex-husband, sitting alone at the bar. How ironic Rachel thought that Allan would be here tonight. She always found him attractive, and lately, since she was no longer friends with Julianne, she thought about contacting him. But how was she going to ditch Tom? Allan hadn't seen her yet, so Rachel grabbed Tom's hand, "Would you mind taking me home?" Rachel asked, trying hard to seem sick.

"Sure," he said.

"Are you alright?"

"It's my stomach."

Tom was afraid to ask anything too personal. He stood up and followed her out the door. Rachel held her hand across her stomach on the way home. She gave Tom a quick peck on the cheek and promised to see him soon. As soon as she got inside the condo, she shut the door and peeked out the window. As Tom's car pulled out of the parking lot, Rachel picked up her phone and searched Facebook for Allan and then messaged him.

Hey, how have you been

hey girl good how are you

fine what r u up to

sitting at the bar at JAlexanders want to join me?

sure see you soon xx

Rachel checked her make up in the mirror before grabbing her purse and walking out the door. By the time she reached the parking lot, Allan was already sitting in his car. Pulling up next to him, she got out of her car and lowered herself into Allan's passenger seat.

They had a long conversation about Julianne. The restaurant finally closed, so Allan drove to the liquor store and bought a six-pack of beer. The conversation continued while they drank the beer. She couldn't believe Julianne would divorce this guy; he was so charming. The feeling must have been mutual; Allan made plans to take Rachel out to dinner the following evening.

If the relationship between Rachel and Allan started as a way for them both to get back at Julianne, then it worked. Julianne heard about it from a mutual friend. She wanted to call Allan and tell him not to even think about bringing Rachel's son around the twins, but she knew if she did, Allan and Rachel would know she was bothered. Julianne knew there was no way she could stop it from happening anyway, so she said nothing.

Allan thought Rachel was a good catch. Rachel lived in a beautiful condo. She split the rent with her roommate, and together the girls could afford a luxurious place. A white leather sectional sat on a plush cream area rug in the living room. In Rachel's room, the bed had an upholstered headboard, and the off-white bedding had a delicate stripe. The building was a new high-rise with a gym on the seventh floor overlooking a patio with a long rectangular pool.

When Allan came over to Rachel's condo, she always looked and smelled her best, and she made sure to have his favorite drinks and snacks in the refrigerator. She wanted him to feel comfortable at her place, so she purchased new pillows like the ones he had on his bed. When Allan showered in her bathroom, Rachel brought him fresh towels. When they watched a movie at his beach house, she always brought popcorn and his favorite Cabernet. On more than one occasion, she made dinner for him from her collection of recipes; Allan loved how domestic she could be when she wanted to. If he left for work before she did in the morning, Rachel would tidy up his bathroom and make his bed.

Allan compared Rachel to the other girls he dated. Most of the girls he found to be controlling and only looking for what they can get out of the relationship. He imagined life with Rachel, and the more time they spent together, the more attached he became.

Rachel even started spending time with Allan's elderly mother, who never got along with Julianne. Rachel took her shopping once a week and spoke to her on the phone every day, listening to the same stories repeatedly.

Men always found Rachel hard to resist, and she had an interesting way of dealing with them. Allan and Rachel began spending every weekend together, and they saw each other occasionally during the week, but some evenings they only spoke on the phone. Allan still liked his alone time and his time with friends. He never wanted to be tied down again. One evening Allan called Rachel to see what she was doing for dinner. He was romantic and always took her to lovely places. When Rachel said she didn't have plans that evening for dinner, she thought he would take her out. Instead, he said he was going out for sushi with one of his buddies, and he would call her later.

Rachel pleasantly hung up and began to form her plan. When Allan finally called her after the sushi dinner, she didn't pick up the phone. He tried calling her cell phone for a while, and he texted her but she never texted him back. Finally, he called the landline at the condo. Rachel asked her roommate to pick up the extension. The roommate pretended she was surprised when Allan asked where Rachel was.

"I just got home, I'm not sure where Rachel went, but she must have just left because I smell fresh perfume." Allan hung up the phone. Where could she have gone? Rachel always answered his calls. He thought he was losing his mind, and he kept trying to reach her all night. Rachel would see Allan's name on the caller

ID, and she was surprised at how persistent he was. She finally turned the ringers off and went to sleep.

The next morning Allan got to work early after barely sleeping. He tried calling Rachel's cell phone and the landline at the condo again. When she still didn't answer, Allan left work and drove over to the apartment. Rachel answered the door and acted surprised to see him. She kissed him hello and rubbed her eyes like he just woke her out of a deep slumber.

"Where have you been?" Allan asked impatiently. Rachel was pleasant and calm.

"I am sorry I missed your call; I ended up going to dinner with a girlfriend from work."

Allan had no way of knowing she had been home all evening. He couldn't be sure if she was telling the truth or not; he thought she could've been out with another guy.

"What girlfriend from work?"

"Lori... I don't think you know her." Allan's head was spinning and he realized that he cared about Rachel a lot more than he initially thought. By the time he left Rachel's apartment to go back to work, he wanted to show her how much he cared for her. He stopped at a jewelry store, and bought her what appeared to be an engagement ring with a cluster of large diamonds in the center. Allan made it clear they were not engaged. He continued to take Rachel on vacation with him and spoil her with gifts.

When Rachel came into the salon for a manicure, she was wearing the ring. She considered it a consolation prize. Her goal was to be married.

"Why not enjoy things the way they are?" I asked.

"Because I have no security," Rachel said.

"And, what would you have if you got married?"

"I would be married."

"But people get divorced every day," I told her, "It's no security."

Rachel had to get used to the idea. Allan would never marry her.

The twins reported everything that happened at their father's condo back to Julianne, and she felt like she was living a nightmare. Allan was the last person Julianne wanted, but why did he have to be with Rachel? Two years after they began dating, just when everyone thought their relationship would not go any further, Allan asked Rachel to move into the beach house. Although he still didn't want to get married, he wanted to be a real couple. Rachel brought her things to the condo on the beach and settled in.

Julianne's ex-friend could have her ex-husband, but the thought of Rachel spending time with her girls was painful; especially on holidays. The twins sometimes felt like they were betraying their mother when they spent time with their father and Rachel. During spring break, the girls stayed at the beach house. Their friends were on the beach every day. One afternoon after they spent an entire week with there, Amber texted Julianne.

can you pick us up

Can't they bring you home?

they aren't here

Julianne wanted to see the girls, so she agreed to pick them up. She had been to the condo before to pick up the girls, but not since Rachel moved in. In the time it took for Julianne to get there, Rachel and Allan arrived back at home. She parked her car outside and noticed both cars in the driveway. She called the girl's cell phones, but they didn't answer. Nervously, she walked up to the door.

Before she could knock, the door opened, and Rachel was standing there.

"Can you please send the girls out?"

"Come in," Rachel said. Julianne reluctantly stepped inside.

The first thing she noticed was a framed photo of her twins and Rachel's son posing with Allan and Rachel on a boat. They all looked like one big happy family. Julianne pretended not to see it. In the kitchen there were items that belonged to Julianne that Allan must have taken from the house when he moved out. She saw an espresso machine that one of her aunts bought her as a gift. Allan was sitting on the sofa watching a football game on television with a drink resting on a glass coffee table that belonged to Julianne's sister. Allan wouldn't even look at her. It was as if Rachel was living Julianne's life. She felt nauseous. Just then, Amber appeared with her backpack slung over her shoulder, with Stella trailing behind.

"Let's go, mom," Amber said, and they walked out the door.

Julianne decided to do a little online dating to forget about Allan and Rachel. While I did her nails, she told me she met a police officer on one of the dating sites. She said she could die now because the weekend she spent with the handsome police officer was by far the best weekend of her life. I laughed, and she proudly pulled up a photo of the guy on her phone. Not the usual type, I thought. Her sisters would never approve of this one, his muscular arms covered in tattoos, and his head completely bald. I was sure he wasn't Jewish.

"Very cute," I told her.

I was excited for Julianne, and I suggested we could double date. I didn't hear from her until her next nail appointment, two weeks later. When she sat down, I asked her how it was going with the police officer. She looked confused for a second.

"It's over," Julianne said. "Russell has been calling me. He left his wife again."

"What happened with the police officer?" I asked. The police officer said he could never be in a monogamous relationship. He confessed that when he was married, he had an open marriage with his wife.

"He's a swinger," Julianne said. I stopped filing.

"He really should have said that on his profile."

Julianne looked up. "That's what I said. Anyway, I told him to lose my phone number."

I finished buffing her nails and began polishing. "I changed my mind," I said. "We are never double dating."

ANN CEDEÑO

CHAPTER 10

Sheila Metzger

SHEILA METZGER GRADUATED FROM LAW SCHOOL, earned her degree, and passed the bar in the state of Florida on her third try, but she never worked as an attorney. Her parents sent her to college, hoping she would meet and marry a husband who could provide the life for her that they anticipated. They wanted her to have a marriage like theirs. Her parents met and married right out of college and had a group of elitist friends. Her father came from money, but it was her mother that spoiled her as a child. Her mother was her biggest fan. Sheila's every wish was her mother's command, and on her birthday, she tired of opening gifts long before she got through the pile of boxes wrapped in colored paper and curly ribbon. Sheila's mother couldn't get enough of her daughter, finding every word she said utterly amusing, leaving Sheila to believe she was charming and brilliant. Nothing could be further from the truth.

In law school, Sheila did find someone to marry her; however at first, her choice for a spouse seemed beneath her father's expectations. Over the years, though, her husband proved to be a great provider, and money was always her father's only measure of success.

Sheila's marriage appeared from the outside to be a perfect union. She was taught by her mother that appearances were important, and that no couples were romantic like in the movies. Sheila felt relevant with all her material possessions, and she was willing to live with a man with whom she had no connection. She never told her parents or anyone else that the marriage has been predominantly sexless for years. Sheila was not a beautiful girl, but her expensive clothing and shoes did make her more attractive.

"Do guys ever come on to you? "Sheila asked me. I was doing her nails.

"What do you mean?"

"You know, if you have workers in your house, do they ever flirt with you?"

"I don't even make eye contact with them," I told her.

I only scheduled a worker to come to my house when my husband or someone else was home, and even then, I was cautious not to be too friendly for fear they would think I wanted them. And I never did men's manicures.

At one time, there was a jewelry exchange next to the salon where a few guys from New York sold 14-karat gold and diamond jewelry. The guys would walk into the salon with their dress shirts unbuttoned enough for their gold chains and the hair on their chest to be exposed. They would walk up to the front desk, gazing past the receptionist, at the young female nail technicians.

"I want that one to do my nails," they would say. Only after each one had picked the girl he wanted would they all sit down for a manicure and close their eyes while the girls rubbed lotion over their hands and down their arms.

It was a tennis pro that Sheila was interested in. She had been taking lessons from him at the club. I should have recognized the signs. First, she lost at least 20 pounds, and was wearing all new tennis outfits, and then she had her teeth whitened. She was sneaking over to the tennis pro's rented apartment whenever she could, but it wasn't tennis lessons he was giving.

Luckily, he tired of her quickly because her life could have been ruined by this infidelity; it turns out, she was not the only one to fall for his tan, muscular legs, and his piercing blue eyes. The pro had an array of married women he sought out to play with. Only after they became attached and mentioned leaving their husbands would he discard them and move on. The women were so desperate to feel loved, they would risk it all. Some were even delusional enough to think that the tennis pro was in love with them. When the affair ended, not by her choice, Sheila gained the weight back and went back to being miserable.

Sheila managed to raise three boys without ever learning to cook, and she didn't know the first thing about cleaning. I always found it interesting that so many of my clients had never cleaned their homes in their lives. Many were busy working or earning degrees for themselves. Their time was rarely spent on such archaic pastimes like cooking and cleaning. Many of my clients have not ever felt the accomplishment of making a house a home nor did their mothers before them. They paid someone to do these seemingly menial tasks, and it allowed them far more idle time than necessary. Without enough to do, many of them got themselves into trouble by spending money they didn't have or involved in an affair that otherwise may have never happened.

Sheila always had a nanny to take care of her children, and when they were small, she had two nannies—one for the weekdays and one for the weekends. She never enjoyed the day-to-day monotony of the children. Every summer Sheila traveled extensively with her husband while the boys were at sleepaway camp. They had no choice but to go for the maximum number of weeks the camp was open. One summer, the youngest boy cried so hard he vomited at the airport before boarding the plane because he didn't want to go, but Sheila and her husband had no intention of canceling their Mediterranean cruise. They kissed him good bye, and handed him over to a camp counselor, before marching out of the airport, and never looking back.

Like her mother before her, Sheila kept busy volunteering to chair one organization or another, and the Diabetes Foundation was her latest endeavor. Planning the 200-seat luncheon took many hours and effort from the volunteers. The event's vendors rented space to sell everything from extravagant art to diamond estate jewelry, and Shelia was in charge of filling up the booths.

Every charity luncheon had an auction. My clients always asked the salon to make a donation for a product or a service. The proceeds from the sale would go directly to the charity. Most of the salon owners I worked for were generous, but often we were simply bombarded with requests for donations. Every week it seemed one client or another had a request for a free service. There were numerous other requests from our clients. Girl scout cookies, GoFundMe accounts, and walk-a-thons were just some of the fundraising events we were asked to participate in. Also, some of the clients got involved with popular pyramid schemes promising to make them instantly rich. The juice that claimed to provide numerous health benefits, liquid vitamins and skincare products were some of the spiels I had to endure during an hour-long appointment.

Once, a client tried to pay for her regular service with me with the gift card I donated to her charity, and I honored it for her because she said she won it herself at the auction. I suppose it was possible.

We also never actually gained a new client from these freebies, although some of the nail technicians donated in hopes that they would. I knew most women had a regular nail technician, and if they did redeem the prize, they immediately went back to their usual tech, with some conjured up story about why someone else did their nails.

Sheila had an air about her that was insufferable. She once told me she stopped recommending me to her friends because I would become too busy, and when she needed to change her appointment, she wanted me to have availabilities for her.

Only Sheila could have the best of the best, and I thought it was fun to watch her squirm when one of my younger clients came in with a new piece of designer jewelry or a Hermès bag that she didn't have yet. One morning I was concentrating on cutting Sheila's cuticles.

"You know the people that live on the water with the yachts?"

"Yes," I said.

"That's the kind of money we have."

I didn't know how to respond. I was grateful when her cell phone rang. It was Emma, a pretty girl who sold handbags and jewelry out of her house. I had been to Emma's home for a fundraiser once. The house sat on an acre of land, and it was such a large residence, I was afraid I would get lost if I needed to use the restroom. The main room where the event was held was cavernous, and beyond that, the kitchen, where the caterer set up, had glass doors overlooking the pool that seemed to disappear when they opened. Emma was raking in cash purely as a hobby; she didn't need the money because her husband was extremely wealthy.

Emma called to say a shipment of fake Gucci T-shirts had just been delivered to her home. Sheila bargained with Emma until she managed to get the $30 T-shirts for $25 if she bought three or more. I wondered why Sheila even wanted the fakes. She had a personal shopper at Neiman Marcus who helped her pick out outfits and handbags. She would call ahead to say she was on her way, and her girl would fill up a dressing room with clothing and shoes. Sheila had no idea where to begin when it came to getting dressed; it was easier to pay someone to do it for her.

On a Sunday around noon, Sheila's black Jaguar pulled up to the valet at Neiman's. She handed the attendant a five-dollar bill before informing him that she had a new scratch on the car, and she believed it happened the last time she was there. He smiled politely and assured her he would give her car the utmost care while parking it in the space only a few yards away.

The salespeople in the store greeted Sheila as she made her way to the contemporary clothing department, where the more casual everyday clothing lined the walls. She didn't glance at any of the clothes as she passed, walking straight to the fitting rooms. Her room was ready with the latest outfits chosen in her size, including a few pairs of shoes to try on to complete the looks. A new Valentino handbag that had just arrived that day hung on the rolling garment rack with the selections of clothing. Her salesgirl promised no one else would be able to get the bag because they were in such a limited supply. The salesgirl knew if Sheila thought it was hard to get, she would buy it. She tried on the outfits but there was a sour look on her face as she examined herself in the mirror.

"Are you sure this brand is still popular?"

The salesgirl would have to convince her to make the purchases. It was only after she would wear the items and people would admire her that she believed her clothing to be the optimum choice, and she always pointed out the fact that she was wearing the latest designer brands in case anyone failed to notice.

Sheila didn't need the fake Gucci T-shirts; she could easily afford the real ones if she wanted them, but I heard her tell Emma she would stop by on her way home from the salon. She never could pass up a bargain, and she would be miserable if the T-shirts were actually of high quality and the opportunity was missed. She asked Emma not to call any of her other friends until after she left; she wanted to be the first to have them.

When she passed the guard gate to Emma's property in a development of palatial homes, torrential rain pelted the windshield. This was common in Florida in the summertime. Every afternoon we would get these storms, usually brief, and the sun would return immediately after. Sheila wasn't about to get wet, and she was thankful for the porte-cochere in the front of Emma's house.

Shelia was furious when she pulled into the driveway. Rosa, Emma's housekeeper, parked her car, blocking the entrance to the porte-cochere. Sheila called the landline to the house, and Rosa picked up the extension.

"Hello," she said.

"Rosa! Its Sheila! Move your car I'm trying to pull in!"

"I will be right out, Miss Sheila."

Rosa ran out of the house, holding a plastic bag over her head. Rosa opened her car door and got soaked by a gust of rain before she could pull the door closed. As she backed her car far enough down the long driveway for Sheila to pull past her in the Jaguar, she cursed Sheila under her breath.

Sheila parked and ran into the house, shutting the door behind her and calling out for Emma. Rosa finally made it back inside, drenched and dripping on the floor. Sheila had a look of disgust on her face at the puddle of rainwater that was collecting at Rosa's feet.

"Get a towel, Rosa! Someone could slip!"

Sheila was a client of mine for over 20 years. In 2017, Angelo and I moved to a new home, and Sheila had recently purchased a home in Aspen around the same time. She hired her designer from Florida to completely renovate the house in Aspen. Every nail appointment as I worked on her cuticles, she fidgeted with her hands, pulling her phone in and out of her bag. Scrolling through the pictures her designer sent her, she always asked for my opinion on them.

"What do you think of this coffee table?" Sheila asked. "This chair or this chair?"

I enjoyed getting a glimpse at the most recent trends and designs; it was like free advice for my new house from her designer. Much like her clothing and her polish color, Sheila didn't have a clue what to choose for her new home. She scoffed at a dark wood table the sought-after designer chose, claiming she already had dark wood in her previous home in Aspen. I thought the dark wood table with its modern lines was perfect in the space that let in so much natural light.

Sheila was having a pedicure with one of my co-workers, and then a dip manicure with me. I have never done pedicures. I preferred doing fingernails only, but I always tried to find the best pedicurist in each salon to team up with so that my clients could have the two services done together. I passed by the pedicure room and saw that she had arrived, so I came over to her with some cotton and 10 squares of tin foil to wrap her nails with; to remove her dip manicure while she was soaking her feet.

Sheila greeted me with a smile, and she pulled out of her bag some swatches for the master bathroom she wanted me to see. They were tiny wood samples for the cabinets. My new home had quartz on the counters in the kitchen and the baths, and the cabinetry was mostly white. My husband and I were excited about our house, and we couldn't wait to move into it at the end of the month. We would be living alone for the first time ever. When we met, I was divorced, and my daughter, Teran, was four. We never had the stage at the beginning of a marriage where it was just the two of us, and we were looking forward to it now.

Shelia wanted a coffee, so I left her for a moment to get it. I cleaned my desk and answered a few texts before making the coffee and adding the two packs of Splenda I knew she liked. As I walked back into the pedicure room, I noticed it had filled to capacity, and I had to maneuver through the tiny rolling chairs the pedicure girls were sitting on to get to her.

The room smelled like lavender from the bath bombs used to sanitize the water. I felt relaxed by the sound of the water trickling into the bowls while the clients with closed eyes were adjusting the remotes on the pedicure chairs to the level of massage they wanted on their backs and necks.

Sheila's head and voice were shaking slightly as she spoke, from the massager. I placed the coffee on the small table next to the armrest. She had the foil on her fingers and the cabinet samples in her hands.

"How much did you pay for your new house?" Sheila asked.

(I hated the personal questions I was constantly asked)

"$745,000," I whispered.

Sheila's voice seemed to become louder, "Do you realize what you paid for your entire house is the same amount I paid my designer?"

CHAPTER 11

Lisa Mitchell

SHARI BECKER APPROACHED THE SALON'S FRONT door for her appointment in a tight maxi dress and five-inch high Saint Laurent platform espadrilles. Somehow her dark hair was still smooth and straight after walking through the 90° heat and 100% humidity. Shari was early, as usual. Bracing her arm on my desk as she slid into the chair, I noticed she was wearing a new Van Cleef bracelet.

"Nice bracelet," I said.

"Thank you! I treated myself after I sold the $4 million house."

The bracelet looked great on Shari, and she certainly earned it. She was a bright young, highly motivated realtor. Her mother had been a client of mine for decades, and she had referred me to her entire 30-something friend group. I was almost old enough to be Shari's mother, and I still remember her as a little girl. In college, she needed a fake ID to get into the bars, and she asked me for my driver's license. I handed it over with one stipulation.

"If you get caught with it," I told her, "You have to say that you found the license."

Shari was always a smart girl and very resourceful; she never got caught even though there was no way she looked 32 at the time. I asked her what her plans were for the afternoon while I did her nails.

"I am working with a couple from Connecticut. The husband's company transferred him to Boca, so I'm taking them to Parkland to see some model homes that just opened."

"I want to see the models!" I told her.

My husband and I were planning to renovate the home we were in, and I needed ideas.

Shari looked down at her phone and started texting with her free hand.

"I made you an appointment for Saturday at 10 a.m."

My husband was always willing to shop for new homes. We had purchased three homes already in Weston. She forwarded the address to my phone.

"When you get there ask for Peggy, she's expecting you."

Shari was going to be in Paris with a girlfriend that weekend. She loved to shop. Hermès bags and scarves were on display next to countless Chanel bags and shoes in her walk-in closet. Designer jewelry and watches filled the narrow drawers. Shari earned every penny it took to acquire these things by selling homes. To be a top realtor in South Florida, you had to be motivated. Every realtor got their real estate license anticipating getting a listing to sell one of the multi-million dollar homes on the water, but not everyone was willing to do what it took. Shari did what it took. I would have gladly used her as my realtor if not for one thing: my client Lisa Mitchell, a close friend, facilitated all our real estate transactions in the past.

I never imagined we would want to buy a house the day we went to see the models, and I planned to tell Lisa all about the new homes in Parkland the next time I saw her. Something about Shari reminded so much of Lisa.

I met Lisa while working in a salon with her sister, Cindy. In those years, Lisa had endless ambition and enthusiasm for her job. When my children were small, Lisa and I sat together on Sundays at Hollywood beach, where Cindy and Lisa's mother owned a condo. Cindy would always get there first with her boys and save us a spot on the sand. We carried our beach chairs and coolers from the parking lot. Cindy's boys had the same blonde curls that Cindy and Lisa had, and it was easy to spot them as we approached the water's edge. All-day long, the kids played together while we sat in the sun. Lisa was married once and had several long-term relationships but never had any children of her own, yet all the pumpkin carving parties and Easter egg hunts were always at Lisa's house. Every year she had a Christmas Party, and "Santa" would hand out gifts to all the kids.

One night at happy hour, Lisa met Ron in the bar of a local restaurant. He was married to his wife for 17 years, and they had three children together. Ron's wife, a plain-looking school teacher, was no match for Lisa. Ron left his wife.

After a short courtship with lots of alcohol involved, Lisa married Ron in North Carolina even though he was not as fit as her usual type. Lisa liked the idea of Ron more than she actually liked him. He was doing well at his job, and he owned a lovely house on an expensive piece of property. The wife would get the house in the end, and much of his earnings would go to child support payments.

My daughter, Teran, and I went to the picture-perfect Grove Park Inn wedding. It was an entire weekend of festivities. The ceremony was on the top of a mountain overlooking magnificent trees, just starting to lose their fall leaves. Nothing was too good for Lisa, she was always a food and wine snob, and she spared no expense that weekend, flying in stone crabs from Florida and serving the most expensive champagne. Lisa kept in touch with all of her exes, and a few of them received invitations to attend the wedding. Ron would have to get used to Lisa's antics. She was not about to give up the friendships of her ex-lovers.

At first, Lisa seemed happy with Ron. They threw parties together at their house after adding a pool with a hot tub and a new custom kitchen. Lisa and I hosted a bridal shower at Ron and Lisa's house. A caterer made Paella in a large wok outside on the patio for the 30 guests. Inside, we made an entire table of appetizers and prepared a full bar. We had no way of knowing that all of the ladies would choose the punch bowl of Sangria to drink. The Sangria quickly ran out, and the little bridezilla was furious, so we began pouring sprite and wine and fruity liquors into the punch bowl with ice. The guests loved the spiked punch, and the shower was a complete success.

Lisa always did what she wanted to do in life, never worried about the consequences especially after her breast cancer diagnosis. Having never had any surgery before, she was terrified when the doctor told her she needed a mastectomy. I drove her to one of her pre-op appointments, and I could tell she was hit hard by the whole ordeal. Cancer can cause you to reevaluate everything in your life and make you realize how short life is. Her eyes were open in a whole new way, scrutinizing everything.

Suddenly Lisa was bored with Ron. Was he gaining even more weight, she wondered? His lengthy conversations about work in the evenings were never enjoyable, and when Lisa gets bored, she cheats. She recently visited an ex who lived in New York. Ron was facing the desktop computer in the kitchen when a photo of a male's private part appeared on the screen. He did a double-take.

"Who is that?"

Ron fully expected Lisa to lie, but instead, she admitted seeing an ex-boyfriend a few times when she was supposed to be staying with a girlfriend in the city. Ron was devastated and wanted to work things out after giving up his family for Lisa. They tried for a while, but Lisa had lost interest in Ron, and eventually they went their separate ways. Over the years, Lisa told me she doesn't know if she has ever actually been in love.

"It's the lifestyle you love," I said.

A life of travel and leisure is what Lisa is looking for, and although she is perfectly capable of providing the lifestyle she wants for herself, she has always been searching for her knight in shining armor. Single once again, she was back to happy hour in the evenings. It was hard to concentrate on business when her future ex-husband may be waiting for her at the bar.

Lisa and my husband had never been each other's favorite people, but they always got along for my sake. After Lisa cheated, Angelo was less enthused with her.

It was a bright sunny Saturday morning when Angelo and I drove up to the community's security gate to see the models. We gave our name to the guard, and the iron gates opened for us to pass through. We parked and walked across the parking lot in the oppressive heat. A professional-looking blonde girl in her 30s greeted us inside the air-conditioned office. She directed us out of the office's back door and onto a path that led to the first model.

When we opened the single front door in the turret entrance, we were instantly in awe of the decor. The finishes were incredible. A winding staircase covered in wood moldings let us from the house's foyer to the second floor where a family room overlooked the lake in the back. A family room on the second floor? The design seemed so different from anything we had lived in before. Off the kitchen was a "casual dining room," which was more practical than having a formal dining room that no one ever used.

We were empty-nesters, and the house was much bigger than we needed, but we could picture ourselves living there. We began referring to that first model as our dream home. The feeling we had was reminiscent of when we were younger and built our first home in Weston, and returning to our own house that day; it seemed inferior by comparison. No amount of renovating would bring our house up to the level of the one we fell in love with, but I was not willing to build another home at this point in my life. Shari suggested we come back. There were a few spec homes of the model we liked that were almost complete.

"What about Lisa?" I asked.

"Don't worry," Shari said.

Shari picked us up the following Saturday in her seven series midnight blue BMW and drove us back to Parkland for another look. While we were driving I asked again.

"What about Lisa?"

"Don't worry," Shari said.

Shari walked into the office of the sales center as if she owned the place. She positioned two chairs for us while we waited for Peggy who was on a call. Shari had a close working relationship with Peggy, and they had mapped out the houses they wanted us to see.

It was easier to see what the house looked like without all the model's upgrades, and the homes they showed us checked all our boxes. One sat on a water lot and had a stunning view of the sunset. After some negotiation, we were ready to sign on the dotted line for the house. We already pictured ourselves living there.

"To do this, we need to sell our house," Angelo said.

Shari pulled a listing agreement with our current address out of her bag and placed it on the table for us to sign. It was no wonder why she sold so many homes. How could she possibly have known that we would list our house that day?

The deal on our dream home was contingent on the sale of our current house. We would only have 30 days to sell the house, and Shari was confident it would happen. Again I asked Shari about Lisa.

"I will be giving you a portion of my commission back, and you can do whatever you want with it. If you want to give it to Lisa, that's entirely up to you."

"Fuck that!" Angelo said. "She didn't do anything!"

Angelo wasn't concerned about anyone's commission; he wanted the new home, and we signed the contract. I waited until the next morning to call Lisa and tell her everything that happened. I was still trying to decipher, where it all went wrong. I prayed she would understand.

"I will give Shari a call and try to work things out," Lisa said. "I am not going to let this ruin our thirty-year friendship."

When Lisa called me back, after her conversation with Shari, she was incensed. Shari told Lisa that no one owns a client, and Shari repeated to Lisa what she told us.

"If they want to give you a portion of the commission I am giving back to them, they can."

Lisa insisted it was not about the money; it was simply that someone else sold us a house. All of her friends and family and co-workers, listened while she told the story of how I, one of her closest friends, dared to use another realtor. Yet, whenever I mentioned moving to Parkland to Lisa in the past, thinking I could live closer to my daughter and her family, Lisa said she hated Parkland. Shari worked mostly in Parkland and had all the connections with the builders there, winning multiple awards for selling her listings.

Still, Lisa expected us to use her if we ever needed a realtor. Disappointment comes from expectations. What about the countless clients I handed Lisa's card to, while sitting at my desk, when they needed a realtor? One year, Lisa's total earnings stemmed from my clients and friends. If it wasn't about the money, what could it be?

I paid careful attention to how Shari did her job. It was easy to see how she made so many sales and won so many awards every year. She always had us leave as she showed our house herself, boasting about the upgrades and getting us top dollar for our home. We had an offer on our house right away that was $32,000 over our asking price. Shari earned her own commission.

When Lisa came in to the salon for her nail appointment, I made sure Shari didn't have an appointment scheduled the same day. Lisa may have ripped her head off if she ran into her. Every chance she got, Lisa brought up how disappointed the real estate transaction made her and how she never expected me to be so disloyal as a friend. I knew Lisa so well. I could feel the hate emanating from her while she had her nails done with me in the salon. Doing someone's nails can be very intimate. As I held her hand, I felt the negative energy she gave off. When I brought up my son's upcoming graduation from college Lisa said, "I hope he doesn't turn out like his father." Hurt people; hurt people. But did the punishment fit the crime? She was treating me like I stole her husband.

Something else was going on in Lisa's life. Cindy, Lisa's sister, was dying from lung cancer, and Lisa was her caregiver. It seemed to me that Lisa and I needed to set our differences aside and focus on Cindy. I went to Lisa's house to see Cindy and Lisa purposely left before I got there. I had no intention of bringing up my argument with Lisa, but Cindy wanted to talk about it.

"I wasn't looking for a house; it just happened," I told Cindy, who was using all her strength not to cough while we spoke.

"I told Lisa to let it go," Cindy said in a deep raspy voice.

When Cindy died, I left work and drove over to Lisa's house. She hugged me, but it felt forced. My daughter and I went to Cindy's funeral, but I knew it was the last time I would see Lisa. I couldn't let her continue to taint the amazing memories we shared. Better to end the friendship before things got ugly. Lisa couldn't let it go. We always had a close bond, but sometimes people can stay in your heart but not in your life.

When Shari and I spoke about Lisa and the transaction, Shari reminded me that she was just doing her job and nothing she did was wrong.

"It's not my fault you aren't friends with Lisa anymore," she said.

Shari got married for the second time and we went to lunch one day in a little Italian cafe in Parkland to celebrate. I noticed the people in Parkland seemed so different from the people in Weston. We were only 20 miles north, but people seemed friendlier and less pretentious somehow. At the next table, we overheard a woman talking to her friend.

"If you shop in the Publix on University Drive and you put a whole pineapple in your cart, it means you are a swinger," the women said.

"I won't be shopping at that Publix," I whispered to Shari.

CHAPTER 12

Dorothy Johnson

WHEN DOROTHY JOHNSON FIRST CAME TO HAVE HER nails done with me, my son was sitting in a stroller. One way for me to figure out how long I have been doing a client's nails was to figure how old my children were when I met them. It's one way we, as moms, measure time.

During Dorothy's first manicure with me, she met a client of mine, Nancy Simons. We told Dorothy I had been doing Nancy's nails since I was 18 years old. Dorothy said her goal was that one day she would also be a long-standing client. She achieved her goal. My son, who was in a stroller when she started with me, turned 25 last year, and I have seen her every two weeks ever since. So much has happened in both of our lives since that first manicure.

It is not uncommon for a client to send their mother-in-law, daughter or mother to me for a manicure. Mother–daughter relationships have always intrigued me; I appreciate a good one. Marge is Dorothy's mother and they have the best relationship I have ever known.

Marge lives in Palm Beach in a historical house the size of a small mansion that she has been living in for 60 years. Once a month, Marge spends the night at Dorothy's, and they consistently have their nails done with me on Friday afternoon during the visit. I pull up an extra chair, and we crowd around my nail table. The two-hour time slot flies by, and we are all disappointed when it's over.

I am fascinated by our conversations. I have never met anyone quite like Marge. When she was young and raising her children, she would dress in the morning after her husband left for work. Then she would wake up her three children, Dorothy and her two brothers, for school. The oldest boy Gene slept upstairs in a two-bedroom apartment with its own entrance. The apartment was added on to the original house years ago by the previous owners when their parents moved to Florida to retire. Besides the two bedrooms, the apartment had a small kitchen and a full bath. Also on the second floor, were four other bedrooms, including the master. On the main level was the kitchen, the living room with a brick fireplace, the dining room and a paneled room with a bar. Dorothy slept upstairs with the family while the youngest, Jimmy, slept in the only bedroom downstairs. There was an unattached three-car garage and a cottage by the pool where Marge's relatives would stay when they came down to Florida on vacation from New Jersey.

Once the children dressed in the morning for school, Marge sat them in the formal dining room for breakfast. A long dark wood table sat in the center of the room under a crystal chandelier that gave off rainbow prism patterns on the wallpaper and the white coffered ceiling when the sun bounced off the crystals. Marge would pack lunches of peanut butter and jelly sandwiches and potato chips while the children ate breakfast and then brushed their teeth and put on their shoes. Out the door they would all go and pile into Marge's new Cadillac. Looking over her shoulder, she backed the car down the long drive, careful not to plow into the mailbox as she had once before. Luckily, Marge had a guy that fixed the car before her husband noticed the damage, but it had nearly cost her a fortune.

To come up with the money to repair the car Marge bought fabric and sewed curtains for her living room, which was no easy task, and told her husband they were custom made by a designer. Marge asked for a check to give to the designer.

"Who do I make it out to?"

"I'm not sure how to spell his name. Just make it out to cash."

Her husband handed her the check, and she used it to pay for the damage on the car. There were two driveways at her house, one in the front, and one in the back. The house sat on a substantial corner lot, and after the car was repaired, Marge could stop hiding the dent by parking next to the bushes in the back driveway.

As soon as the kids hit the door of the school, in the morning, Marge made a beeline for a local dive bar on the beach. She peeled off her dress in the broom closet, and stepped into her cocktail waitress uniform. All day she served drinks at the bar. Tourists flocked to the beach looking for a drink before breakfast, and Marge was there to greet them. Her husband thought she still worked as a secretary, but her boss had fired her for taking one too many long smoking breaks.

"I didn't go home until I found another job," she told me. "I don't understand how the kids today say they can't find work." With her tips, Marge was making three times what she made as a secretary. Her husband didn't keep tabs on her money. She paid for all the food in the house, and after shopping for the groceries, she stashed what was leftover in a coffee can in the pantry.

In the afternoons, after the lunch rush, Marge put her dress back on and hung up her uniform. She picked up the kids and drove back to the house. She waited for the familiar knock on the back-screen door, and Mr. Nathan, who owned a nearby restaurant, showed up each night during the week with dinner. After dumping the plastic containers of food into her everyday china, she served it to her husband and the children as if she had been slaving away at the stove for hours.

Dorothy remembered the parties on the weekends at the old house. The solid wood bar with low lighting off the dining room was the perfect backdrop for a party. On these nights, Dorothy's father was always the one behind the fully stocked bar at the house, and Dorothy loved how her father let her stir the cocktails after he made them, with a tiny straw. The parties would still be going on when Dorothy fell asleep upstairs, and occasionally the music would wake her. By the time she woke up, in the morning, she wasn't sure if the sounds she heard through the floor the night before were real or part of a dream.

It wasn't surprising that the marriage didn't last. Marge felt like a rebellious daughter instead of a wife, and eventually, her husband found out she was working at the bar. Dorothy heard her parents fighting through the walls of the house after the boys were fast asleep. Marge asked her husband to leave.

"Without me, you will never be able to keep this place," he said. Years later, she was still proving him wrong. Dorothy got married and left the house at 23 years old. Then her brother, Gene, moved to Georgia where he worked for the phone company. Jimmy moved to New Jersey after he graduated high school, but his marriage only lasted a year, and then he moved back home. Marge began renting rooms to people she came in contact with at the bar. Only single tenants rented the rooms. Some ended up staying for years.

Marge told the tenants not to bring much when they move in; she furnished everything, including dishes and towels. They only needed to bring clothing and toiletries. There was never a lease of any kind on the rooms.

"That way," Marge said, "I can tell them to leave whenever I want. If I'm not happy, or they aren't happy, I don't want them in my house."

There hadn't been a mortgage for years on the old house, but it still cost plenty to live there. The money Marge earned from the renters paid the taxes, but when the homeowner's insurance increased to over $10,000 per year, she cancelled the policy. Needless to say, she did not allow candles in the house and when there was a hurricane, she prayed all night that the whole thing didn't blow away.

The house, as big as it was, always needed constant maintenance and was always undergoing improvements. The lawn was mowed and the pool was cleaned every week. The pool was like a pool at a resort. Marge had it built after her husband left. The pool ended up to be over eight feet deep. While the pool was being built her son Jimmy was selling the dirt and pocketing the money.

A reliable man who could fix things for her was the ideal tenant, so she traded rent on one of the rooms for services. It should have been a good deal for both parties, but more than once a handyman took advantage, embezzling extra cash from Marge when buying supplies. Only once a tenant stole liquor from behind the bar.

Marge's house parties became much smaller, but they still went on, and the bar was stocked in case an impromptu get-together happened. At one such gathering, Marge noticed her bottles were nearly empty, and she started to mark the level of the spirits to determine who was around when the levels dropped. Once she figured it out, the man responsible had two days to find a new place to live. She had no problem being stern when she had to be, and if Marge ran into trouble with a tenant, Jimmy would step in. Jimmy lived in the three-car garage that Marge renovated to be yet another apartment for income. Dorothy thinks her brother resides there for free, but at least he keeps their mother safe.

Marge always asked me about myself and she seemed genuinely interested.

"Why don't you do pedicures?" Marge asked.

"I prefer doing manicures, and none of the owners ever had a problem with it," I said. Then I told Marge about a girl I worked with named Lucille, who stopped doing pedicures at Indulge Me.

The pedicure room has become a relaxing haven with dim lights and the sound of running water from a free-standing water fountain hanging on the wall. But, in the 80s, the pedicure room was a constant buzz. The lights were bright, and women could barely keep their feet still to be polished while they squirmed in their chair talking over each other. From the main floor of the salon, cackling laughter could always be heard.

Lucille had her client Beverly's heavy leg propped up in the air while she was slicing away at the skin on Beverly's heel with a tool that's now illegal to use. It was a handle with a straight razor that cut through callous like a cheese grater through a wedge of Parmesan. The skin was flying and Lucille started to laugh at something she heard, and when she did, she sucked her breath in, and somehow a little piece of the dead skin from Beverly's shriveled white calloused heel flew into Lucille's mouth and down her throat. Lucille stood up with her hand over her mouth, and ran to the bathroom to try to dislodge the skin, but when she tried coughing, the skin only slipped further down. Lucille never did another pedicure after that. We were the only two nail technicians who got away with only doing nails.

Marge always had new stories for me about her tenants. She had rules, and she swore she didn't allow any drugs near her house. She had a tenant in the cottage outside that drove her around after she stopped driving herself. It was a good arrangement; the man didn't have a car of his own so Marge let him use hers, and he took her to the bank and the grocery store. She continued to let him drive her car after he lost his license. The man was pulled over and the police found a bag of pot in the car. Marge told me the pot wasn't his. It was adorable the way she defended them like they were her children.

Marge had always saved money and purchased stocks in her grandchildren's names. Somehow, she talked the tenants into saving money. Each week when they gave her part of their paychecks for rent, she asked for an additional amount to invest for them. The tenants received statements every month, and they saved more money than they ever had before.

The tenants sometimes asked for an extension on the day rent was due and Marge trusted them to pay her the next week. She used to stay up until midnight, sitting in her chair at the dining room table but as she got older she started retreating to her room before 8 p.m.

"I don't go right to sleep," she said. "I just rest my eyes." The tenants who were late on rent seized the opportunity to leave unnoticed with their belongings during the night, never to be heard from again.

On Marge's 90th birthday she threw a party for herself outside by the pool. She made her famous potato salad and catered a barbecue for everyone. Her son, Gene, hired a band and set up a keg of beer. Marge's granddaughter, Tammy, came down from New Jersey for the party. She never knew Marge growing up. Her father, Jimmy, left her mother while she was pregnant with Tammy. What a shock Tammy got when she came searching for her father a few years ago, and she found this amazing grandmother in the process. Marge had Tammy's picture hanging in her house, and she seemed sad to have missed out on so many years with her granddaughter.

I often told Marge about my grandmother. We call her "Granny." She is the same age as Marge and owns a condo in Boynton Beach. Her condo is decorated with antiques that she had in her previous house for years and her marble floors are covered in colorful oriental rugs.

When I visit my grandmother, we have tea and tiny sandwiches in her living room. From my spot on the sofa I see the community pool surrounded by bottlebrush trees. Granny's little dog, Rex, a terrier mix, sits next to me while she tells me stories of the family from before I was born.

I can tell that Granny thinks about the stories she wants to tell me before I visit and she has photos laid out on the Lucite coffee table to help me visualize the people she refers to. It's warm and cozy on the sofa and I feel so comfortable there, I almost fall asleep. When I have to leave, I consider she will be alone again when I drive away.

Granny hugs me good-bye and always hands me a toy for my grandson, Jace as I get into the elevator. Jace is Granny's great-great-grandson. I am a grandmother and I still have a grandmother. I feel very fortunate.

I compare Marge to my grandmother. They are both really something for their age. I notice how Dorothy looks at her mother with admiration, and I wonder if they know how rare it is to see a mother–daughter relationship this good. When I talk to Dorothy alone, she tells me she would love for her mother to come and live in her big house; she has plenty of room. Or, Marge could get a condo like my grandmother that she could take care of by herself. Marge told me she would die if she ever had to leave the big house and live like an old person alone in a tiny condo.

"The house keeps me going," Marge says. I guess it does, she just turned 94.

CHAPTER 13

Olivia Gallo

OLIVIA GALLO WAS RUSHING TO GET TO A YOGA CLASS when her mother stopped her at the front door.

"Do you have anything for pain?" Olivia turned around and quickly walked down the long hallway, scattered with family photos, pulling up her long brown curls into a bun as she went. Opening the top drawer of her tall dresser, she grabbed the pills and came back down the hall where her mother was waiting.

"I will be back after my class," Olivia said. She shut the door behind her. Olivia's mother had a doctor's appointment scheduled for Monday, still three days away. Her arm had been hurting, and she hoped the pills would help her sleep. When Olivia got back from her class, she heard the faint sound of the water running in her mother's shower. She hadn't eaten anything since lunch. She opened up the refrigerator to look for something light. A blueberry yogurt sat on top of a Tupperware container filled with penne ala vodka from the night before. Since her older sister moved out, and it was just the two of them, Olivia and her mother didn't cook formal dinners every night. One of them would prepare chicken for a salad or a pasta dish, and they would have it for lunch or dinner the next day.

Olivia chose the small container of yogurt and sat down at the kitchen table. When she lifted the last bite yogurt to her lips, it occurred to her that her mother should have finished showering by now. Olivia stood up and walked through the living room to her mother's bedroom door. Standing in the doorway, she could see the light coming from the bathroom. Olivia knocked.

"Mom?" There was no answer.

Olivia slid the bathrooms pocket door open and saw her mother lying on the floor. The pills were on the edge of the vanity, and her toothbrush was still in her hand. She ran to get her cell phone to call 911. When she returned and bent down to look at her mother's face, she knew she was gone. A neighbor saw the ambulance and came inside with the paramedics. The neighbor knew Olivia and her sister, Michele since they were babies, and she adored their mother.

"Let's call Michele," the neighbor suggested. She helped Olivia up from where she was seated on the floor. As soon as she heard her sister's voice, she began to cry, and she could hardly speak.

"You have to come over. It's Mommy," Olivia said.

Michele lived nearby with her husband and new baby boy. Grabbing the baby and throwing him into the car seat, Michele rushed over and immediately took charge. Olivia relied on her older sister to decide on funeral arrangements for their mother and then list the house they grew up in for sale.

"This house is too big for you," Michele said. Olivia could have easily bought her sister out with her share of their mother's life insurance. Still, the electric bill alone on the house would be more than she made in a week at the busy chiropractic office where she was the receptionist. Instead, Olivia used her portion of her inheritance to buy a smaller house a few streets away. The house had blonde wood floors and new white kitchen cabinets. Some of the homes in Hollywood, built in the 70s, were newly renovated, and this one had a new air conditioner and a new barrel tile roof.

Michele only took a few precious items from her mother's house. Everything else she left for Olivia. The dining room table that the entire family spent every holiday sitting around became where Olivia sat in the mornings when she drank her coffee. The six matching chairs, covered in a silk vintage patterned fabric, looked beautiful in the bright sun-filled room. She picked the most worn chair to sit in, convinced it was her mothers. When she sat in the chair, she could feel her mother's presence all around her. Little reminders of her mother were everywhere. She kept the silver grapefruit spoons with the serrated edge that her mother used every morning in the silverware drawer where she would see them. Next to her bed was a family photo of her parents and her sister from years ago. The girls were mini versions of their mother with brown wavy hair and fair skin.

When the girls emptied their mother's bedroom, they found her diary. When she was ready, Olivia planned to read the entries her mother wrote in her perfect handwriting. Having her children later in life, their mother always tried to prepare them for her death, knowing they might still be young. Michele was 37, and Olivia was 34 when she passed away.

After eating oatmeal a few nights in a row, Olivia stopped at the Italian market to pick up some fresh mozzarella. She had been craving the soft white cheese for days. Dressed in a pair of loose jeans and sandals, Olivia wondered if Gino, the owner's handsome son, would be there. Gino flirted with her every time she saw him. Too bad he was so young, or she may have teased back.

As Olivia walked through the doors of the market, the cold air felt good on her skin. Florida residents tended to forget how hot the summers were while enjoying the perfect climate in the winter. She picked up one of the small baskets in the entrance and filled it with tomatoes, basil, and a loaf of fresh Italian bread to go with the mozzarella. Walking through the produce, Gino spotted her before she saw him, and he walked over to say hello. She didn't remember him being so tall, and he must have been working out; his arms seemed so muscular. His hair was long, almost to his shoulders, and he pushed his bangs aside as he offered to ring up the items in her basket. When he finished ringing up the order, he asked Olivia if he could have her phone number.

"How old are you?" Olivia asked.

"Old enough," Gino winked. "I will be 24 next month."

Olivia's tiny frame and small features made her look much younger than she was. No one who saw them together would suspect he was ten years younger, and what did she have to lose? He handed her his cell phone, and she entered her number.

He texted her as soon as she left the store.

Hello beautiful

Olivia went home and prepared the basil, sliced the mozzarella and tomatoes, and took out the olive oil and balsamic vinegar to drizzle over the top. She poured herself a glass of wine and sat down and for the first time since she lost her mother, she felt content.

Gino's family worked long hours in the store, and besides running the market, and making fresh baked goods, he and his parents had a catering business. Olivia texted him back. He happened to be getting off early that day.

When are you free?

I just made fresh pastries

If you let me come over

I will bring you some

A guy who makes fresh pastries? I have to see this, she thought, and she texted him her new address.

Gino ran home and took a shower and pulled up to Olivia's house in his white Porsche Carrera with a bottle of wine and an entire box of assorted fresh pastries. Olivia was impressed. She guessed the store must be doing well if he could afford the car he was driving.

"Did you shower?" Olivia asked. The ends of his hair were still damp.

"I didn't want to smell like garlic."

Pulling two wine glasses out of the cabinet and setting them on the counter, she started searching for her wine opener. Everything in Olivia's house was neat and organized. She remembered she moved the opener earlier that day to the drawer next to her small wine refrigerator. As soon as she picked it up, Gino grabbed it, covering her tiny hand with his enormous fingers. He opened the wine bottle effortlessly and poured them each a glass.

Holding her wine glass in one hand, she carefully sat on the sofa, and she motioned for Gino to join her. He asked her why she didn't have a boyfriend, and they talked about her recent breakup. She dated a guy named Anthony for three years who turned out to be very immature.

"Why don't you have a girlfriend?" Olivia asked. Gino seemed to squirm in his seat.

"Do you have a girlfriend?"

"It's complicated," Gino said.

"How complicated?"

Of course, Gino has a girlfriend, Olivia thought. Not only did he have a girlfriend, but she was also living with him.

"We can be friends, right?" Gino asked. Olivia thought about it.

"Sure, we can be friends."

After Gino left that day, he started texting Olivia non-stop and would stop by after work with dinner and wine from the market. He was thoughtful and romantic; everything she wanted in a man. Olivia had convinced herself that Gino was no longer in love with his girlfriend, and she allowed herself to fall for him. Maybe Gino was the one.

Olivia was curious about Gino's live-in girlfriend, so she decided to stalk him on Facebook. She hadn't been on in a while, and she missed a ton of messages about her mom. Friends posted pictures of her mother and tagged Olivia and Michele. Gino's page was mostly pictures of him by himself. She requested to be friends with him and then logged out.

A month later, after spending more and more time with Gino, Olivia popped into the market one day, unannounced. She didn't see Gino, but she saw his mother helping another customer. She wandered around until the customer left, and then she made her way over to the counter.

"Is Gino here?" Olivia asked, feeling self-conscious as his mother looked her up and down. Maybe it was her imagination, but Olivia could have sworn she saw his mother roll her eyes. His mother answered sternly in her heavy Italian accent.

"He's not here," she said. Then she walked away. When Olivia got to her car she texted Gino.

What is wrong with your mother?

She is very protective of me

How does she know about us?

I tell her everything

Gino was a mama's boy. He often brought his mother to the salon for facials and pedicures, and clients commented on how adorable they were together. Olivia knew she needed to make a good impression on his mother, but it was not easy. Staying away from Gino until he broke up with his girlfriend was the right thing to do, but it was impossible. Did Gino's mother know how persuasive her son could be with women? When Olivia finally distanced herself, he planned his next move carefully.

Early in October, Gino pulled his work truck into Olivia's driveway one afternoon and waited for her to come home. She wasn't expecting him, but her heart leaped when she saw him sitting there. Maybe he broke up with the girlfriend, Olivia thought as she pressed the button to open her garage door and pulled inside. She stepped out of her SUV, but Gino was still sitting in his truck, so she approached the driver's side window. Something was on his lap, and it was moving. It was a miniature Pomeranian puppy named Cannoli. Carrying him inside, Gino handed him to Olivia. Cannoli slept in Olivia's arms while Gino explained he was going on a guys' golf trip at the end of the month. He planned to break up with the girlfriend before leaving, so she could move out while he was gone.

It was finally happening, Olivia thought. Soon we will be a real couple, and we won't have to sneak around. That night they slept together in Olivia's bed with Cannoli between them. Gino got up around 3:00 to go home. Why was Gino still worried about going home if the relationship was over?

Olivia was awake, so she checked Gino's Facebook page. Gino still had not accepted her friend request, but the page was public, and she could see every one of his posts; pictures of him at the beach, at a baseball game, and a photo of him posing on the golf course. His most recent post was of him in his car with a girl. The girl tagged him in the picture. Dina? Who was Dina?

But, true to his word, the girlfriend was gone when he got back from his trip. Gino wanted Olivia to come over to his house the next weekend. He picked her and Cannoli up after he closed the market.

Gino's house was four times the size of Olivia's. She was not expecting the 2-acre lot it sat on in the exclusive gated community. The back yard had a pool and a fireplace. She could get used to spending time at his house. Thanksgiving would be the first time she would meet Gino's entire extended family. He was planning to host the holiday.

Michele was disappointed that Olivia was not coming to her house for Thanksgiving dinner, but Olivia promised to go over the day before and help her sister cook some of their mother's favorite recipes. Olivia hesitated in telling Michele about her new boyfriend. She knew what Michele would say; any guy who cheats for you will cheat on you, but she was happy for Olivia when she told her she was seeing Gino. It bothered Michele when she thought of her sister at home alone.

Olivia knew Gino was catering one night, and when he didn't answer his phone, she assumed he was busy. She tried texting, still no answer, so she tried to sleep. The next morning Gino texted her while driving into work.

Hello beautiful

What happened last night

Sry working late went home to crash after

Olivia was trying not to be insecure with Gino. She knew he had a lot on his plate, so she never made demands, but she couldn't help wondering if he always told the truth. She noticed he never put his phone down. He even took it with him to the bathroom. Gino told Olivia he was going to New York for a week before the holidays. He had cousins who live in the city, and he visited them when he could. He barely had time to text while he was there.

The day before Thanksgiving was one of the busiest days of the year at the market. Gino would be there all day and into the night. Olivia left her house to drive over to her sister's and spend some quality time with her. Michele helped her choose the perfect dress to meet Gino's family. Olivia ultimately wore a plain black v neck dress. It was classic, but it still showed off her figure. Michele and Olivia spent the entire evening preparing their mothers recipes, drinking wine, and reminiscing. Cannoli was on the floor, and the baby was in the high chair next to them. The baby never cried until his father scooped him up when it was time for bed. For the first time in her life, Olivia thought she wanted a baby of her own.

Olivia got up at 7:00 the morning of Thanksgiving, and threw on a pair of sweatpants with a matching jacket. She packed a bag with the dress and her makeup for later and threw it into the car along with two flower arrangements, one for the table and one for Gino's mother to take home. Cannoli was still asleep in his little crate, so she picked the whole thing up and buckled him into the passenger seat. Traffic was light, and when she pulled up to Gino's house, he came out to help her with her things. Gino thanked Olivia for the flowers and the tiramisu she brought.

"It was my mother's recipe," Olivia said.

Folding tables and chairs sat in the living room. Stacks of linens and trays of food were on the dining room table. They would have to get to work quickly to have everything ready by 4:00. Most of the food was prepared the day before at the market and would only need to be heated later, but there were appetizers to prepare. Family members were in and out of the house all day, dropping off their contributions to the dinner.

Olivia, tired of being caught in her sweatpants, finally went into the bedroom to do her makeup and hair and slip into her dress. Gino's mother showed up at 2:00 and started undoing everything Olivia did. She didn't like the placement of the silverware, or the glasses set out on the bar. She saw the flowers and held them up.

"What are these?"

Olivia could hear them. Gino whispered for his mother to stop. What was her problem with Olivia? By 4:30, the entire family showed up. Gino said there would be 37 people, but with the children, it was more like 50. Olivia's feet were already killing her. She went into the bedroom to slip on her sandals, and no one noticed she was gone. Gino was too busy to introduce her to anyone. Olivia recognized Gino's aunt and cousin from the store, and they smiled when they saw her.

"Sit with us," Gino's aunt said. Olivia sat while Gino stood at the bar, drinking with his brothers and cousins. Olivia wished she was anywhere else but there and felt relieved when everyone left. On the way out the door, Olivia heard Gino remind his mother to take the flowers, but she left them behind. When Olivia asked why his mother was so cold to her, Gino said it was her age.

"She wants me to be with someone younger."

"Doesn't it matter what you want?" Olivia asked. Gino was looking at his phone.

"If I am your girlfriend, age shouldn't matter." Gino looked up.

"Olivia, I can't commit to you right now. I just got out of a serious relationship."

Shocked by his statement; Olivia grabbed her bag and Cannoli and walked out the door. Gino let her leave. She assumed they would be a couple after he broke up with his live-in girlfriend. She waited for him for months, and he never even took her on a real date. Now he wants to be single? Unable to stop the tears from rolling down her cheeks the entire next day, she waited for his call. Finally, he texted her the usual.

Hello beautiful

hello

do you miss me

yes

do you want me to come over

yes

An hour later, Gino pulled into her driveway, and Olivia opened the door to let him in. He came bearing gifts; bones for

Cannoli and a bottle of wine for Olivia. Leaving it on the counter, he led Olivia down the hall. Gino was the type to solve everything in the bedroom.

Gino continued to text Olivia, but he was busier than ever during the holidays. When he did come over after work, he was so tired he would fall asleep.

"After all the parties, I will have more time," he promised.

The chiropractic office where Olivia worked had a holiday dinner every year at The Capitol Grille. Each employee was invited with a guest. Olivia asked Gino to join her.

"Babe, I'm sorry, but I am catering that weekend." And what could she say?

Olivia came into the salon to have her hair and nails and done. I put red gel polish on her nails to match the new red dress she was wearing to the party. Cora, her friend from work, picked her up. Cora didn't have a date either, so they decided to drive together. The girls at work knew Olivia was seeing someone special, but they had yet to meet him. After a few drinks, Olivia told Cora who she was seeing.

"I know his mother, Marianna."

"You do?" Olivia asked.

"Yes. She's best friends with my aunt. Isn't Gino like 20 years old?" Olivia laughed.

"He's 24."

Since he was so busy, Olivia helped Gino by doing his holiday shopping for his entire family and then wrapping it all and putting it under his tree. While she wrapped the gifts, Gino was working. Olivia loved to wrap gifts; it reminded her of when she used to wrap gifts late into the night with her mother and sister.

On Christmas Eve, Olivia went to her sister's house early in the day. She planned to spend the night so she could watch her nephew open his gifts in the morning. Gino spent the evening at his parent's house, but he promised to come over Christmas night.

Olivia realized she missed her period. What if she was pregnant? The pill made her sick, so Gino was extra careful. She didn't mention her missed period when he came over to exchange gifts with her, but she didn't have any of the champagne he brought to share. Gino began opening his presents from Olivia. There were six packages, perfectly wrapped. She put a lot of thought into each gift. She bought him a wallet, sunglasses, cologne, and three of the Robert Graham dress shirts he liked. Then it was her turn, and she expected her gifts to be over the top, knowing how much he spent on his family. He got her the same thing he got his three nieces—a pair of yoga pants from Lululemon. He had to leave early that night, he was going out with some friends, but he promised to text her when he got home.

"You can come over after if you want to," Olivia said. When she woke up, there was no sign of Gino, not even a text. She had enough of his games. How hard is it to text to say that you made it home?

Olivia assumed she would be spending New Year's Eve with Gino, and she bought a new outfit when she was shopping for Christmas presents. It was a pair of dark skinny jeans and a halter top. Trying it on in the mirror, she realized her breasts seemed swollen, and they were sore. I hope I'm getting my period, she thought.

New Year's Eve day, Gino told Olivia he had other plans for the evening. She was furious and told him never to call her again, and she meant it. It wouldn't be easy, but she had to let him go. She sat home and watched television that night. She didn't hear from him all night or the next day. When he finally texted her, she didn't respond. After a few days, he became desperate, sending a guy over to her office to wash her car and leaving little notes in her mailbox.

Olivia finally stopped at Walgreens to get a pregnancy test on her way into the office. The suspense was killing her. She felt like she was about to get her period, but it never came. She went right into the bathroom at the pharmacy and pulled the stick out of the box. Now that she finally bought the test, she couldn't wait until she was back at the office to see the result. Within seconds the test showed positive. Olivia put the stick back into the box and dumped the whole thing into the garbage.

The office was full of patients when she got there. The other girls were buzzing around. Maybe if she didn't think about the test result, she could get through the day. She knew she needed to tell Gino. There was no way she would have an abortion, so it looked like she would be having a baby on her own. Just then, Cora came around the corner holding a patient's file.

"Come here for a second." Cora said. Olivia followed Cora into the break-room. Cora shut the door.

"My aunt told me that Gino is getting engaged." Cora said.

"To who?" Olivia was trembling.

"To a girl he has been dating who lives in New York. She was here for the holidays, staying at his mother's house." Olivia was in shock. Cora said Gino had been seeing her for a year, and that's why his live-in girlfriend broke up with him.

"That explains a lot," Olivia told Cora.

"I just wanted to let you know, so you don't waste any more time with him." Too late for that, Olivia thought. Gino started texting as usual in the afternoon.

Hello Beautiful do you miss me

do you call your fiancé beautiful

what?

meet me at my house at 5

k

When Olivia saw Gino's face, she knew it was true. They sat on the sofa, and Olivia started to cry.

"I'm sorry," Gino kept saying.

"Why did you keep seeing me if you knew you wanted to be with her?" Gino tried to explain. She was a 21-year-old virgin who both families expected him to marry. She was inexperienced and never worked a day in her life. Gino said he loved the girl, and wanted to marry her, but he also loved Olivia and couldn't imagine his life without her in it. Then she told him about the baby.

"Please don't ruin this for me, Olivia."

"What do you mean?"

"If her family finds out you are pregnant, they won't let her marry me." Gino's words were crushing her, but he held her tight.

"I will make this right, Olivia, I swear. You and the baby will never go without."

Gino married the girl from New York two months before Olivia had the baby. The wedding was at the Biltmore Hotel in Miami, and afterward, they spent their three-week honeymoon in Greece.

The night the baby was born, Gino told his new bride he had a catering event. He was by Olivia's side while she pushed their baby into the world. They named her Jeanie after Olivia's mother. If Gino's mother knew about the baby, she never said a word, and Gino kept his promise. He visited the baby when he could, and he deposited money in an account every week. He was generous; Olivia was able to quit her job at the chiropractic office. She no longer needed to work, and she stayed at home to raise Jeanie. Gino even had a pool built in Olivia's backyard when Jeanie was three and learned to swim.

Olivia was playing with Jeanie and Cannoli late one afternoon when she received a text from Gino.

Hello beautiful do you miss me

yes

I'm on my way over with dinner.

CHAPTER 14

Linda Goldstein

WEDDINGS HAPPEN EVERY WEEKEND IN SOUTH Florida but never without endless trips to the salon first. Salon employees hear all about the pre-wedding family drama during the trial hairstyles and trial manicures. My client Linda Goldstein who came in every Tuesday morning, was planning a wedding for her son, Jacob. Linda was extremely demanding and had a strange obsession with anything purple. Her nails were often a shade of purple, and her home had purple accents scattered throughout. Her wardrobe included purple clothing and designer bags, and even a purple leather jacket.

Planning a wedding is supposed to be pure bliss. Two families are joining together, full of love and hope for the future, or at least that's how the story goes. But in reality, pressure can slowly build-up, and words get spewed like hot lava with no filter and are impossible to take back. Forget what the bride wants because it's not her wedding. It's all about the mothers; it's their chance to shine, and no two women are ever alike. Even if their religion, education, and upbringing are the same, each mother has her own vision of how this five-hour celebration should unfold. Luckily for Linda, who was very controlling, the bride's mother was not in the picture. Linda saw this as an advantage, not having to share the wedding planning with another mother. Jennifer Bloom was only eight years old when her mother died. Her father, who was quite a bit older than her mother, raised her by himself.

There are always several mini celebrations before the big day. Engagement parties measure how frugal or extravagant the families are willing to be. Money always seems to be an issue no matter how big or small the parents' bank accounts are, and wedding etiquette is interpreted differently depending on who it benefits—kind of like the Old Testament.

I heard clients say, "I hope they know that the groom's family is supposed to pay for the engagement party, and the flowers, and the band." And, "Can you believe his mother isn't going to get centerpieces for the rehearsal dinner?"

Jennifer's father set aside enough money to plan a tasteful affair. Shopping for a wedding gown is one of the bride's first outings once a couple announces a wedding date. The dress will set the tone for how formal the wedding will be. Mothers and daughters have bonded over this shopping excursion forever. Asking the future mother-in-law to come along is an honor and a privilege. The bridesmaids often join them and give their opinion on which style gown suits the bride the best.

Jennifer was missing her mom when she arrived at the boutique to pick a gown, but Linda was there, already selecting dresses when she walked in. Champagne was served by the bridal salon to evoke a party atmosphere in the dressing area made of mirrored walls. Endless yards of white silk and tulle and a thousand dreams filled the space.

Linda's controlling personality could have ruined the day. The bridesmaids were rolling their eyes at her. She had an opinion on everything. Still, Jennifer welcomed the help, having never planned an event before, and she knew one of the wedding colors would have to be purple, Linda's favorite color. The bridesmaids were not thrilled with the purple dresses Linda chose, but Jennifer thought they were fine.

Jennifer and Linda went to every wedding vendor together. Nothing in the budget was good enough for Linda to present to her group of friends. The centerpieces for the reception included in the package Jennifer's father chose were not what Linda had in mind; they were too ordinary. She complained to her husband, a senior partner in a large law firm, who threw money at the problem. It was as simple as writing a check to the florist and ordering more purple flowers. He spent all of his time at the office but knew how to keep his wife happy, and the florist promised purple flowers and red roses in full bloom would cover every surface in the room.

The only time the bride challenged Linda was over the music, wanting a DJ instead of a band. Linda said if Jennifer weren't careful, she would choose a white gown to wear to the wedding and show up the bride. Impossible, I thought; the bride didn't even need Botox yet.

During cocktail hour, guests balanced sushi rolls and crab-stuffed mushrooms on tiny plates resting on little purple cocktail napkins with the wedding date imprinted in silver. The caterer set up a colossal ice luge sculpture next to the bar. Vodka ran down the center of the ice over the bride and groom's initials.

The wedding party looked stunning. The bride walked down the aisle like a princess in a Vera Wang halter gown. Linda wore a plunging lavender floor-length dress. The florist didn't disappoint; the centerpieces held plumes of fresh flowers cascading above the guests' heads during the reception, where everyone danced all evening. The entire room had dim lighting casting a soft purple glow. Next to the valet at the end of the night, a man in a tuxedo offered cappuccino sprinkled with chocolate powder and paper cones of warm chocolate chip cookies. A heavenly aroma was in the air. Linda seemed satisfied that her guests were impressed with the details of the party.

Jennifer and Jacob's marriage had none of the components it needed to last. The first problem was that Jennifer was not in love with Jacob. He had been a rebound. When Jennifer met Jacob, she was still in love with Mark, a guy she dated for over three years. If it were up to Jennifer, it would have been Mark she married instead of Jacob. Everyone close to Jennifer was happy when they finally broke up; Mark was a bit of a loser, never finishing college. After Mark cheated on Jennifer with one of her friends, Jennifer never saw or heard from him again.

It was evident that Jacob was the better choice for a husband. He came from a better family, and Jennifer knew she would have a comfortable life. Although Jacob had no interest in becoming an attorney like his father, he went to law school and passed the bar because that's what his parents expected. Jennifer thought if she tried hard enough, she could fall in love with Jacob, but that's not how love works.

The second problem was Linda. She was a nuisance with all her good intentions, and Jennifer was not used to being micromanaged. The house they moved into was the one Jacob's parents wanted them to buy, one they could be proud to say their son and his wife lived in, but the payment was more than the young couple could afford.

Linda insisted they all have dinner together every Sunday. At one of the dinners, she announced she was getting a new car and that Jennifer could have her old one. A four-year-old Lexus was much better than the Honda Jennifer had since high school. The inside of the car smelled like Linda's perfume. Rolling the windows down, the smell of the perfume lingered and the musky scent gave Jennifer an instant headache. She ripped the purple refillable water-bottle out of the holder as soon as she got home and tossed it into the trash.

Less than a year later, Jennifer was pregnant with her first child. Linda seemed slightly offended at the unfairness of it all.

"I don't want to be a grandmother yet," she said.

I wondered what she expected would happen after they were married. Linda had settled into a routine, and she was content with her life just the way it was. Her husband left for work long before she woke up, hardly ever getting out of bed before 10 a.m. With the house quiet, she enjoyed coffee in the morning. Alone time was crucial to Linda. She played tennis at the club most days, showering there before having lunch with her friends. On the weekends, she and her husband always had reservations to go out if they didn't plan to go away for the weekend. She had no intention of giving it all up to babysit for Jennifer and Jacob. The thought of being called Grandma made her eye start to twitch. Linda's mother has been called Bubbe, and she certainly wasn't going to be a bubbe.

When Jennifer came home from the hospital with the baby, they named Sam; she had postpartum depression. Jennifer had a hard time bonding with Sam. He cried all day and didn't want to eat. Jacob was no help, working long hours at his father's law firm. He came home to dirty dishes and bottles in the kitchen sink, and the two began fighting. Jennifer tried to explain to her mother-in-law that she was having a hard time, but Linda only wanted the best for her precious son and she had no patience for Jennifer.

"You need to get up and put some makeup on and take care of your son," Linda said. She hated going to Jacob and Jennifer's house. It was always a mess, and she couldn't stand to look at it. Linda's house had always been spotless, and she always managed to look presentable. Jennifer tried to pick things up if she knew anyone was stopping by, but Linda liked to pop in on her unannounced. There were so many baby things; it was impossible to keep them all neat. Bottles and pacifiers were drying on the counter, and diapers and wipes sat in several locations so they would be easy to find. A swing, a baby seat, and a stroller sat in the living room next to the clean laundry that needed folding.

Jennifer couldn't keep up, and she needed a break. She began to leave her responsibilities to go out at night. Only when Jennifer went out and drank with her friends could she feel better about her situation. Jacob tried to keep the outings a secret. He knew Linda would never approve of Jennifer going out at night by herself, and he didn't want to hear what his mother had to say on the subject. Jacob hardly minded Jennifer leaving. It gave him a chance to work on the script he started to write years ago. Writing was his passion, and there was no time to devote to it, working all day at the law firm and then coming home to help with the baby.

Jacob hoped things with Jennifer would work themselves out, but they continued fighting all the time. Taking care of the baby was not as hard as Jennifer made it seem. In the evenings, while she was out, Jacob put Sam in a baby sling across the front of him while he wrote, and Sam slept the entire time; the warmth of Jacob's body and the clicking of the keyboard lulling him to sleep. Jacob was more worried about telling his parents that he wanted to quit working at the firm and start writing full-time.

Sam was very thin, and Jennifer said he refused to eat. The doctor diagnosed Sam with a sensory disorder that made eating difficult, and he wasn't getting the nutrients he needed. If he didn't start eating soon, he would need a feeding tube. The stress was too much for a new marriage with so many obstacles already. Linda was very critical of Jennifer and blamed her for not being a good enough mother, and she started to ignore Jennifer and only call her son at work to ask about the baby. After being stuck in the house for days, Jacob got home from work, and Jennifer handed him the baby.

"Your turn," she said, and she walked out the door. Jennifer was leaving the house by herself more and more frequently. One night she ran into Mark, her ex-boyfriend. It was bound to happen; Mark was always hanging out in the bars downtown.

He had always liked to party when they were dating, but he only smoked pot and did a little cocaine from time to time. Then he was prescribed painkillers after a car accident and became addicted. He offered Jennifer a combination of drugs, and she swallowed them with the beer she was drinking.

Jennifer finally got home at dawn. Walking into the house, she felt like she was walking into someone else's nightmare. It smelled like baby powder and formula. The air was still, and the toys that Sam didn't seem interested in peppered the floor. Life with Jacob and the baby had not turned out the way she expected. Life seemed to have let her down in general. When she was pregnant, she pictured herself playing with her baby all day at the beach, as her mother had with her when she was small. Because of his sensory issues, Sam hated the feel of the sand, and he cried whenever she tried to take him.

Jacob woke up that morning late for work with Sam in his bed. He had three missed calls from his father. Walking into the living room, he saw Jennifer lying on the couch. He was angry with her for being out all night but relieved at the same time that she made it home. Always in the back of his mind was a fear that something would happen to her. Many nights she stumbled in the door after drinking with her friends.

"Where were you?" asked Jacob.

"With friends," Jennifer said.

"Nice of you to come home."

Jacob left for work, and Jennifer fell into a deep sleep. When she woke up, the phone was ringing. It was Linda calling, and she sent her call to voicemail. Linda called Jacob at work. He admitted that Jennifer was out all night with friends the night before.

"Married women with a new baby do not stay out all night with friends," Linda said.

Jacob knew he would never hear the end of it.

Seeing Mark made Jennifer feel like herself again, and the pills he gave her got her through the days. On Sam's first birthday, Jennifer didn't want to have a party, but Linda insisted. After all the gifts Linda bought for her friends' grandchildren, it was time for her to collect. There was tension between Linda and Jennifer, even though Linda tried to act like everything was fine in front of the guests. She regretted the day her son married Jennifer. Nothing was going according to her plan.

Sam's little arms looked like strings hanging from the sleeves of his T-shirt at the party. He was so tiny compared to the other babies, and he hadn't started walking yet. Jacob sat Sam in a high chair, where he stared at the ceiling fan the entire time. Around and around, he watched the slow, unsteady fan pass. Linda tried to engage him, but Sam wasn't interested in her. He screamed and held his ears when everyone started singing "Happy Birthday" to him, and finally, Jennifer picked him up to take him home. Linda tried to stop her.

"You can't leave. It's his party!"

"He doesn't like all the people and the noise, Linda." But Linda didn't understand. She thought Sam's strange behavior was all Jennifer's fault. Jacob defended Jennifer when Linda called that evening.

"Leave her alone, Mom."

"It must be something she's doing," Linda said. In comparison, all of Linda's friends' grandchildren seemed to be outdoing Sam, which frustrated her.

Alcohol slightly numbed the pain Jennifer felt, and before long, she was drinking every day, and Jacob noticed her behavior starting to change. Who could blame Jennifer? She watched Sam, hitting his head on the floor of his bedroom, and she felt no connection to him. Maybe things would have been different if

Jennifer's mother was still alive; her mother may have been able to give Jennifer the strength she needed.

Jacob, on the other hand, was a wonderful father. Jennifer watched him with Sam, and she envied his patience and his calm demeanor. Jacob seemed to accept Sam exactly how he was, and the love he had for him was endless.

Sam continued to miss every milestone. At his two-year-old checkup, the pediatrician said he should have 50 words in his vocabulary. He wasn't speaking at all, and the doctor sent Jennifer and Jacob to see a specialist. After a series of tests, Sam was diagnosed with autism.

That night after the appointment with the specialist, Jennifer needed to go out for a while. Jennifer didn't want to think or talk about Sam and the diagnosis. She met friends at a bar, and after a few drinks, she relaxed.

Sam was enrolled in the nursery school at the temple with all of Linda's friends' grandchildren, but after the diagnosis, his teacher explained that the school was not the right fit for someone like him. Linda was outraged. She had donated money to the temple's building fund for years.

"How dare they turn him away!" Linda said. But the small private school did not have the resources to help Sam. He would always require special programs. Linda was in complete denial, and she found a therapist to come to the house to try to help her grandson. Jennifer listened from the next room to the therapist, but it was clear that Sam wasn't responding. Jennifer went into the kitchen and poured herself a drink.

During the day, Jennifer would disappear for hours, leaving the house filthy. Linda had no patience for the way she was acting. Jacob could not continue to take care of the baby and work all day while Jennifer behaved like a single girl, partying with friends from God knows where. Linda was not about to let Jennifer make a fool of her son. Jacob begged his mother not to get involved in his marital problems, but enough was enough. Linda arrived at the house, ready to confront Jennifer. Her car was in the driveway, but no one answered the door. Linda called Jacob at work from her cell phone, and he came home from the office.

"One of her trashy friends must have picked her up," Linda said. "You need to divorce Jennifer."

"Jennifer moved out yesterday," Jacob said.

Jacob sat his mother down and told her that he was leaving the law firm. He hated every minute of working there. The screenplay he was writing was coming along, and the more time he had to devote to it, the better.

"Your father will be furious!"

"He already knows Mom, and so does Jennifer." What would everyone think? Linda was only concerned with appearances.

"I want to sell the house and stay with you and Dad for a while."

"What about Sam?"

"I am keeping Sam with me until Jennifer gets her shit together."

There was plenty of space in the house, but Linda did not see herself living with a small child at this point in her life. She started to make arrangements, hesitantly at first. Her cleaning girl would need to start coming in three times a week instead of just once. The home gym Linda had installed in Jacob's old bedroom during a recent renovation would need to go, so Jacob could sleep in the room. Sam could sleep in a smaller bedroom down the hall. His toys would fit on shelves inside the closet. Linda and her husband hoped the living situation would be temporary. Maybe Jacob would meet a nice girl and move on with his life. Jacob had full custody of Sam, and Jennifer only had supervised visitation, which she rarely took advantage of, although she lived only a short distance away with her father.

Jacob never returned to work as an attorney, but five years later, his screenplay was almost finished. Sam was in a school that suited his needs, and he was making some small improvements. Sam still didn't speak, except for a few words, and one of them was Meme. It was Sam's name for Linda. Every afternoon Linda greeted Sam when he got off the school bus and made him a snack while his dad was busy writing. Sam was learning to communicate from his iPad, where he touched the phrases he wanted to say. Sam shared Linda's love for anything purple. He had a collection of purple bears, which he lined up in his bed. Sam only wanted his Meme to tuck him in at night.

CHAPTER 15

Stacy Newman

STACY SAT DOWN AT MY STATION. IT WAS THE FIRST time I met her, but she was a salon client for years. She was very open with me and talked about her marriage as if I already knew her. It was a second marriage, not so unusual, I thought. It was not that she had an affair with a married man while she was married; that happened many times before. It was that Stacy and her second husband had six children between them and the youngest boy and the youngest girl, both 23 years old, recently fell in love. When she told me, halfway through her manicure, I was shocked.

"You know I'm writing a book about my clients," I said.

"You can use it," Stacy said.

There were so many issues with the relationship between the step-siblings who were thinking of getting married. I needed time to process. The other siblings would now be siblings and in-laws?

Stacy will have to share her daughter with her husband's ex-wife, who will be her daughter's mother-in-law? The holidays should be interesting. Stacy and her husband have no children together, but they may share grandchildren one day with each other and with their exes?

Diaries of a Nail Technician Volume 2 will tell the entire story of Stacy. I need time to get to know her.

ACKNOWLEDGMENTS

To all my friends who became my editors, Dody Katz, Nancy Simons, Robin Chess, Julie Hallman and Laurie Tepperberg, I am forever grateful. To the youngest, and most precious editor, Samira Masri, who read my stories, gave me feedback and encouraged me to keep going, thank you so much.

I am always thankful for my husband, Angelo Cedeno, who handed over his laptop every day so I could write. Without Grammarly and Book Baby this book would also not be possible. I really should have paid more attention in school.

Salons having to close during Covid-19 allowed me the time needed to hide myself away and write. It is amazing what can be accomplished when given such an opportunity.

ABOUT THE AUTHOR

Ann Cedeno lives in Parkland, Florida, with her husband, Angelo. Their son, Angelo, who lives in Nashville, is a drummer for the band Southpost and is an avid reader like his mother. Their daughter Teran lives close by and has blessed Ann and her husband with a son-in-law, Jeremy, and a grandson, Jace. Ann's family all patiently listened as she talked about being an author, only half believing she would actually do it.

Ann always felt she was born to do nails, and she has enjoyed her career immensely because of her clients. In fact, she still works as a nail tech to this day in a salon in Weston that her close friend, Kelly Riccelli, owns and operates.